Naked in
Deccan

Naked in Deccan

Venkatesh Kulkarni

A Novel

Stemmer House
PUBLISHERS, INC.
Owings Mills, Maryland

Inquiries should be directed to
Stemmer House Publishers, Inc.
2627 Caves Road
Owings Mills, Maryland, 21117

A Barbara Holdridge book
Printed and bound in the United States of America
First Edition

Library of Congress Cataloging in Publication Data
Kulkarni, Venkatesh
    Naked in Deccan.
    "A Barbara Holdridge book."
    I. Title.
PS3561.U444N3   1983   813'54   83-9190
ISBN 0-88045-030-4

Dedicated to
A beautiful West Virginia lady, my spiritual friend,
Margaret Raine Preston, "Peg,"
A great and noble teacher, Richard P. Adams,
Mentor and personal inspiration of my life, André Malraux,
Symbol of Kannada literature and its nobility, Manvi Narsing Rao.

Contents

PROLOGUE
Deccan   13

PART ONE
  1 *Untouchable*   17
  2 *Octogenarian Goat*   25
  3 *Young Goat*   33
  4 *Beautiful Woman*   38
  5 *Village Robbed*   45
  6 *Countryside in Modern Times*   52

PART TWO
  7 *Master*   61
  8 *Man and Wife*   67
  9 *Trustee*   73
 10 *Traditions*   79

PART THREE
 11 *Little Prince*   87
 12 *Turnabout*   93

PART FOUR
13 *Ganga*   105
14 *Separation*   108

PART FIVE
15 *Sons*   113
16 *Hiatus*   117
17 *Revelation*   119
18 *Seduction*   120
19 *Rebel*   122
20 *Solution*   124
21 *Extinction*   127
22 *Temple*   128

PART SIX
23 *Monsoon*   133
24 *Havoc*   134
25 *Naked in Deccan*   141
26 *Finale*   149

I would like to express my indebtedness to the following works, and to express my gratitude to the following persons: K. Santhanam and R.S. Mugali working for the Gandhi Peace Foundation, New Delhi, and R.R. Diwakar for Bharatiya Vidya Bhavan, Bombay, for Janna's classic poem, *Yashodharacharite;* and A.A. Macdonell of the Association Press, Calcutta for his *Vedic Mythology.* These works have also been reprinted in various standard anthologies.

deccan

The area is called Gudur-upon-Bhima. The land is thin, the rivers are rocky, the villages are sparse, and the people are mostly lean. The landscape is dotted with meager huts and old abandoned mansions, and lined with stretch marks of fate masquerading as cart-driven paths deeply embedded in the dark earth.

The story is that of a lonely, vast, dark and immutable countryside, in our own time. A railroad station serves a small market town and a huge countryside. The railroad station is a watering place for all the steam engines that carry trains from Bombay to Madras and back.

A mansion stands ten miles away from the railroad station, on the banks of the river Bhima. The village of Gudur surrounds the Mansion. Besides Gudur, there are three other villages that dot the landscape between the Mansion and the railway station. The most populated of these villages is that of the Harijans—the children of God, or the untouchables—and is called Kusumurthy. In Kannada the word means "a child's image."

There is one other village in that stretch of ten miles, but there are no people in it. Only roofless houses and strange memories abound in this ghost village by the river bend. The people in the countryside have named it Kalla Halli, "the Village Robbed." As time passes, the other villages are close to becoming ghost villages too. But there are some people who have never left the land, and never will.

Thimma is one of them.

Part One

1

untouchable

I CANNOT LET THIS BOY ROT with you, Rama!" the Master thundered. "The caste system will bury him beyond redemption. I must lift him up *now*. How come he knows so much? Particularly so much mathematics?"

In his youthful eagerness, Thimma answered the question faster than his father. "I studied up to the fourth grade, sir!" he said.

"Under whom, boy? I did not think anybody would want to teach an untouchable."

"Under old man Shamsar Ali, sir. The old Muslim from the railway station."

"You mean to tell me you studied under the same man who was my tutor before I went away to Gulbarga High School and Osmania University? The bearded mullah who taught me so much good Farsi, Arabic and Urdu; who taught me so much philosophy and mathematics?"

"The very same man, sir. He said it was the kindness of your mother that had made it possible for him to open a school under the banyan tree near the mosque. It was the great dowager who gave him the money. On that raised platform we had a huge blackboard and several wooden benches. The upper-caste boys sat on them. All my friends from the villages: Hanumanth Rao of Badyal, Jimkala Mallanna and Police Marya. And the old man's own children, Usman, Husain and Abbas."

"And he let you, an untouchable, study with them?"

"They sat on the high platform. I sat below close to the earth. They sat on the bench. I sat next to the cowdung. That was sufficiently proper for the villagers. They didn't mind. And the irony of it was, sir, I could hear the teacher better than them."

"If you know about ironies, you are ready to be uplifted, boy." The master laughed. "This land of ours abounds in ironies."

Thimma's enthusiasm was on the rise. "He taught me what he knew, sir," he said. "A little Farsi, a little Arabic, some Urdu, some Hindi, and a lot of Kannada—language and literature."

"Good God, man! The teacher seemed to have favored you over me! He never taught me Kannada. What else do you know, boy?"

"Not much else, sir," Thimma said, using his already masterly ability to combine humility and deception.

"You want to study some more, son?"

Thimma's hopes rose high. He always liked the work of the mind. He wondered if this would be his one chance to get away from digging the long mud waterway for his father's rice fields, day after day. He wondered if he was going to be uplifted today. Only a divine miracle would make it possible. "I am a believer," he said to himself.

Thimma's father intervened. "No, Master, he can't. He shouldn't. We need him. I need him. He's my only son. He's my property. He's my asset. He needs to go to work. That's why he's building the waterway."

"What a waste of a fine human being with an excellent mind! Any fool can dig that ditch, Rama! Don't make this poor boy's brains fall into it. No! No! I'll not have it. I'm sorry, I can't let you do that. I must use my authority for some good. That should be the only purpose of authority in this human world of ours; the power to do some good. I am going to find your son an occupation where he can use his brains."

"I'll not protest, Master. But he must have his rations for the year. What I mean is he must feed himself. He cannot be a burden on me."

"Don't be so hypocritical, Rama! You are a Madiga, the lowest of all the untouchables, but you are doing better than most of the upper-class people in your village. Didn't you lend twenty bushels of corn at thirty-seven percent interest to that middle-caste Police Mallanna, that octogenarian goat?"

"I thought no one knew that, Master. I cannot imagine how it came to your attention."

"Listen, Rama! When a cat drinks milk it always closes its eyes. And it thinks the world cannot see what it's doing. I know what goes on around here. A master must share only one quality with God, the father. He must see everything and he must ignore most of what he sees. I don't mind. You are cutting in on my lending to the villagers. But I do not have enough grain to lend to all the people who need it. I thank you for trying to feed them. Oh God! If most of them would only work. The lazy louts. That's a dreaded disease in our country. Indolence. I only hope you have better luck in collecting your debts than I have had with mine. And watch out that the upper-caste people don't pull rank on you and then cheat and default on you. No matter how well you are doing, you are still an untouchable. If you complain to the police, the police will never back you against an upper-caste defaulter."

Rama's sunburned face and hollow cheeks became grim with determination.

"I know, Master," he said. "But the bottom line still is that I am a better farmer than any one of *them*. We untouchables have always been closer to the land than any of the upper-caste people. Every year they consume more corn than they can produce. Every year they need more than they make. So they must cooperate or else! Or else this untouchable will see to it that as the new years come by, their festivals—their Dussehras and their Deepavalis— are going to be empty. They will have to pay for their previous deceptions, in interest and in agony."

Now he smiled a cunning smile. "That's all, Master," he said, with a knowing look.

The Master enjoyed, appreciated, Rama's cleverness.

"Rama! You have the low cunning of an untouchable. In a prince such cunning would be called masterly statecraft. What's your boy going to do? Follow in your footsteps?"

Rama was uncertain. "I don't know, Master. All that schooling has turned his head. Now he works in the fields only when I insist upon it. When he goes home, instead of feeding the bulls and cleaning the barn, he wastes precious time and more precious kerosene oil reading all kinds of books." A certain pride animated the father's voice now, as he talked about his son's "delinquency."

"One day he proceeded to explain the meaning of Lord Krishna's life to *me!*" he said.

The Master laughed. His stentorian voice was like the majestic Deccan thunder. It reverberated across the farms. And finally it seemed to drown itself in the distant Bhima river.

Thimma identified the Master with all the central elements of nature—the sun, the rain, the thunder; Surya, Varuna, Indra. The

Master was the representation of God in the Deccan. God the father.

"What's your name, boy?"

"Thimma, God. I mean, Master."

"They call him Sali Thimma, Master," Rama said. "The Thimma who went to school. The other kids in the village think he's a wise guy and they set him apart."

"There's nothing wrong with that, Rama." The Master looked at Thimma with great affection. "He looks as if he could be head and shoulders above the others. He has personality. Let me tell you something about the caste system, Rama! If he were a Brahman he would have been called Vishnoo, the great preserver of the world, the god of love and money. But because he's an untouchable, even his name *has to* indicate the 'proper' inferiority of his caste. The Madiga's god is Thimma and the Brahman's god is Vishnoo. They are the same deity, but they cannot be worshipped in the same way!"

The Master walked towards the river. Rama and Thimma followed him.

The Master's voice echoed back from the river. Thunderous. Majestic.

He told Rama what he was going to do. "I'll take him into my house. I'll put him in charge of some business. I'll see what he does. I want to bring young boys from all castes into my household. I am going to build a new society with this new generation."

Rama was skeptical. "Will they accept an untouchable as a supervisor over them? These villagers here think us the lowest of the low, Master!"

"Let them challenge me, Rama!"

The Master's mind went back to the event of his father's gruesome assassination, the assassination that had taken place six months before he was born, in 1908. How did it feel to be fatherless in the Deccan? Very lonely. He had never seen him. And neither had Rama. But his mother, the widow, had taken Rama under her wing, hadn't she—in spite of all the trouble she had had to go through with the highly offended Brahmans who had openly threatened to expel her from the Brahman community?

The Master spoke to Rama. "My mother took you under her wing, didn't she, in spite of all the trouble she had to go through? And look where you are now! From a sharecropper to a landowner! Not bad, I say!"

"We are still not very rich, Master," Rama said evasively. He really did not want the Master to know his exact financial situation. "We must give up the clothes on our back so we can own some land."

"I know what you are saying, you low-caste devil! Do you think I really have the baseness to take advantage of anyone, let alone an untouchable? That goes against the whole tradition of my family, the principles of my caste. No, greedy man! Have no fear! I'll not take advantage of you. Your son will be assigned specific emoluments. Thirty sacks of grain and one hundred rupees for one year's work."

Rama was elated. Overjoyed. He had made his point.

"That's more than fair, Master. That's generous. No one in the countryside would consider giving a sixteen-year-old boy such wages. *I* wouldn't do it."

"But *I* must. He deserves it. I have great faith in him."

Thimma liked the Master. He liked his aphoristic talk, his generosity. This was his man. For Thimma the world consisted of teachers and students; the people who knew and the people who were learning to know. That's how Indian civilization, his civilization, had survived for 3,000 years and more. That was probably the basis for the system of hierarchies that Indian society was and probably always would be. The ancient scriptures said, *"Matro Devo Bhava! Pitro Devo Bhava! Guru Devo Bhava!*—Mother is the image of God! Father is the image of God! Teacher is the image of God!"

Rama spoke. "Master, as the river is my witness, from this moment my son is your son. You become his father. He comes under your shadow."

Father and son prostrated in front of the Master. But their hands did not touch the Master's feet. They touched the Deccan earth. They were untouchables.

In his heavenly, thunderous way, the Master commanded Thimma.

"Come and touch my feet properly, boy! Does a son ever shrink from touching his father's feet? There can be no respect without affection, son!"

Thus Sali Thimma, the schoolman-untouchable, joined the staff of the Master.

So did two of his three classmates from the old Muslim's school.

One was Hanumanth Rao of Badyal. His father, the leader of a large middle-caste clan, said, "I named the boy Hanumanth Rao after the monkey god, Hanuman, who was a disciple and a servant of Rama, the sixth incarnation of the Lord God Vishnoo, and who, according to *Ramayana,* after helping Rama build the stone bridge across the Indian Ocean, led the monkeys on behalf of the Supreme God, and destroyed Ravana, the emperor of evil."

The Master appointed Hanumanth Rao of Badyal his new manager of the household, the home minister, as he called him. The Master told his wife, in a late-night conference in the third-floor bedroom of the Mansion, "He's the leader of the toughest clan in the area of Gudur-upon-Bhima. His closest cousins number over a hundred. The best thing you can do with a clan is to make sure that it never gets out of the system so it can oppose it. You co-opt it. That's why I have made Hanumanth Rao the new household manager, a position of great trust. Also because he's basically a very honest, dependable and loyal boy, though not as intelligent as Thimma. He's going to supervise the farms, the farming, the cleaning of the great Mansion, the tending of the great courtyard and the garden, the upkeep of the artesian well, the maintenance of the outside office that I have given to the local teacher for his elementary school, and the perpetual cleaning of our nine-chamber outside latrine."

His wife blushed a little. The Master continued. "It will be his job to arrange for the whitewashing of the Mansion every Deepavali, our annual festival of lights." The Master really enjoyed his Deepavali, the festival that occurred during the Indian winter harvest; the holiest and the most festive of all the festivals. He looked forward to it every year.

The Master appointed young Jimkala Mallanna—the man who had been named after the fast-disappearing Deccan deer—his new treasurer; the finance minister, as he called him. Mallanna's job was to store the grain in a huge seven-storied, underground, perpetually descending earthen granary. It was also Mallanna's job to measure and to weigh the grain periodically, and to arrange for a caravan of bullock carts to go to the merchants at the railway station of Krishna-upon-Bhima, every summer and every winter. These caravans generated periods of great Deccan conviviality and bonhomie even though their economic value was not so considerable. The land did not produce that much. But they marketed what they could. In the winter it was rice and wheat and soya beans. Year round it was tobacco and chilies and corn and tamarind.

The previous treasurer of the Mansion told young Mallanna, "You better watch the tobacco carefully, son, because every year, without fail, half of it disappears among the peasants who drive the caravan to the railway station." Mallanna knew that would not be an easy task. He would have to oscillate continually between empathizing with the destitute and pathetic peasants and being loyal to his Master, who demanded some semblance of order and method in the distribution of the meager produce of the land.

Thimma's job was neither that of a manager nor that of a treasurer. He was generally referred to as the "son" of the Master.

The untouchables asked Rama what his son was doing for the Master.

Rama said, "In everything that has to be done, Thimma always has the largest share. He loves to get away from farms and farming as if all that I taught him is worth nothing at all. He advises the new treasurer, young Jimkala from the upper caste, on techniques of storing and distributing, and most important of all, on organizing the long caravan of bullock carts that are borrowed from every villager who is prosperous enough to have one." Rama had made sure that no one, not even Thimma, knew that he owned a bullock cart. He had made arrangements for his bullock cart to be legally in Hanumanth Rao of Badyal's name.

In the villages an untouchable became prosperous by making everyone think he wasn't.

Rama's younger brother, Soma, who had three children of his own who were not getting anywhere, spoke up. "Your son has the great ability to talk to anyone on any subject and convince him that *he* has a willing ear. Remarkable how, on the surface, he violates no rules of caste propriety, no niceties. I have seen him work. Even when a higher-caste person asks his advice or begs *him* to intercede with the Master on some legal or economic matter, Thimma always manages to show deference to the petitioner; the supplicant. Always he sits on the ground near the chicken coop by the village school or the huge, ancient, famous wooden log near the cattle shed, where the bulls make such a mess, while the *petitioner* sits high on the stone platform by the artesian well."

"That's my Thimma," said Rama, with great satisfaction and pride. "If young Jimkala Mallanna gets advice from him on economic matters, Hanumantha Rao of Badyal "('who has legal title to *my* bullock cart,' he thought to himself)" counts on Thimma's advice on everything else, big or small, including the right quality of whitewash to be bought for the Deepavali whitewash of the Mansion."

Rama's brother, Soma, said, "I am quite jealous. Very. My sons are nothing more than village goondas. They have come to believe that an untouchable can do no more than that in the Deccan."

2

octogenarian goat

ROM AMONG THIMMA'S FRIENDS of the Muslim's school, the only
one not to join the Mansion's staff was Police Marya.
Police Marya belonged to the same caste as Hanumantha Rao of Badyal and Jimkala Mallanna. They were all of the
subcaste of cane-gatherers, people bound together like sugarcane
sticks. Still Marya could not, and did not, do what the others did.

That was because of the *other* Mallanna in the villages,
Marya's father, the octogenarian goat, Police Mallanna.

Presiding over his personally owned cockfight arena, the octogenarian goat, Police Mallanna, shouted, "I cannot stomach the
fact that young Jimkala Mallanna, who has been given his name
after the disappearing Deccan deer because of his mild manner
(and let me tell you, in my book all mildness is the same as
effeminate sissiness), should become the treasurer of the Mansion,
particularly considering how young he is. That's turning the world
upside down; I mean having a buck occupy one of the oldest offices
in the Deccan. After all that sonofabitch is only my son's age! Why
him? Why not me? *I* was the one who contributed most to the coffer
for the Master's father's assassination. I *handled* the money.
Shouldn't I have been the one?"

In the Deccan, perverse logic did not startle too many people.
They had seen enough peculiar turns in their 3,000-year-old history.

The object of Police Mallanna's anger and hate, the man
named after the disappearing deer, young Jimkala Mallanna, the
new treasurer of the Mansion, was deferential as always. "My
consolation is that old man Mallanna hates me the *least* of all
people. One must be grateful for little mercies that come from
people of wealth. I only wish God hadn't decreed that the old goat
and I have the same name."

Jimkala Mallanna's neighbor in the cockfight audience joined

25

in the discussion. "What is Police Mallanna's significance to the Deccan land? Why is the old goat so consequential to us?"

"Because he's haughty. He's arrogant. He makes himself powerful by his looks, his deeds. He has a handlebar moustache. He is thin as wire. He wears, always, an immaculate purple silk turban. He keeps six mistresses. And he is one of the sixty people who contributed money to the assassins' fund for the murder of the Master's father long ago. All that adds up. His health, his lust, his pride in his clothes, and his contribution to various immoral causes have a cumulative effect on the villagers."

Jimkala Mallanna's neighbor could not be convinced. "Your namesake is the Police Patel," he said. "As the man in charge of law and order in the village he always wants to assume power and exercise it; but he just does not seem to know how. Forever he is boasting; talking of his six mistresses and his powerful cock; but people pay him no more serious attention than they do to his cocks here."

"I don't know," Jimkala said sadly. "The Master's father *was* killed, six months before he was born. And Police Mallanna contributed directly to that serious situation with the power of his money."

"But what about today? Mostly his wild stories are causing nothing more than a charitable giggle or an occasional untouchable's derisive laugh. Neither his mahogany stick nor his silk turban seemed to have helped him in asserting his authority. Over the years Police Mallanna has come to resemble the gigantic painted wooden statue that he bought at the village fair a few years ago."

"From the rich proceeds of his illegal hashish profits."

"The statue always blinks, bless its poor, non-existent heart, but we all know it has neither vitality nor will. Even the one great deed of the old goat's life—his contribution to the assassins' coffers —that he committed to instill fear of him in us hasn't done the trick. The Master, born posthumously, the only son of the murdered Prince, is at the helm of affairs, as his father was earlier."

"He lacks the moral force," Jimkala Mallanna said. "The moral force that is a combination of real power and a genuine awareness of justice for others and justice for oneself."

"And who, who indeed, can take seriously Police Mallanna's *new* caste system!"

"You mean his single social idea according to which he wants everyone in his caste, and in castes lower than his own (including the untouchables), to bow down to him, but he will certainly not bow to the Master himself? This great social philosopher of ours wants the caste system to reach *up* to him but not go above him."

"I heard that!" Police Mallanna shouted, immediately stopping the cockfight. "Your new power has gone to your head. You talk nonsense. Goddammit, when will you realize that the equality of cocks that is democracy has come to India again? Yes, yes, yes! The equality of cocks is here. And according to the new democracy; according to this new cock equality, every caste above the level of my caste that is thirty-second in the hierarchy has been leveled. Yes, sir, thirty-two steps are no more. But every caste below my caste has to remain where it is because that, *my dear inferiors*, is your destiny. According to the new rules promulgated since 1947 it has been clearly established, in court and in parliament, that my cock is as big if not bigger than the Brahman's, even if not as intelligent as his. That much of equality has to be there. Otherwise what's the use of having the new freedom; the freedom from the Britishers; the old dictators? But make no mistake. Let no sonofabitch, particularly an untouchable sonofabitch, even dream that a caste lower than mine is equal to mine; a prick lower than mine is equal to mine. That cannot be; that'll never be. I know. I should know, shouldn't I?"

"We don't know," the audience egged him on. By this time the tension caused by the cockfight being stopped had subsided.

"Yes, I should know," Police Mallanna reassured himself and his audience. "I have seen turns of history. I've created a few; among the Deccan women; among the *contours* of our history."

"That we know," the villagers laughed.

"I know. I have lived four score and more years. You all know my theory. You all know Police Mallanna's theory," he said, now assuming the royal third person. "According to Police Mallanna's theory, he is equal to the Brahman, but the Madiga—the untouchable—is not equal to him! Now or ever!"

"Now you know why I went to work for the Master," Jimkala Mallanna told his neighbor. "Is it so hard to understand why Police Mallanna does not have what he always wants so badly? He can never possess moral authority, no matter what he does."

But moral authority was not everything in the villages. Everyone knew that Police Mallanna's sexual powers, his great cock, remained very strong. And had been strong for a long time.

At sixty-three Police Mallanna fathered Police Marya, who grew up to be a hefty, strong, 300-pound, six-foot-six wrestler, who could climb the greased pole at the village fair faster than anyone else.

The villagers said, "Marya is a monster of a man, a straight descendant of the mindless giants who were God's opponents in the story of the *Ramayana!*"

Bully that he had trained himself to be, Police Marya beat up every kid who got in his way.

However, he never touched Sali Thimma.

Marya did not want *his* hands to be soiled by touching an untouchable.

But after school he always got as far away from Thimma as he could and hurled vicious, thick globs of spit at the untouchable's face, while daring him to do something about it.

Thimma always wiped his face off quietly with the edge of his torn brown dhoti, and walked away.

The other untouchable boys hated Thimma for doing that. They resented his humility and his ability to withstand humiliation.

"We want to rise up as one and fight the middle-caste Marya," they yelled around Thimma. His cousin, Taaya, said, "Going to school has made you a sissy, a weak one, a feminine!"

"You read a book and you cut your thing off," Ranga, Taaya's younger brother, joined in. "What's the matter with you, boy, you influenced by them Kristen missionaries who have come across the river or what? They converted a whole village of untouchables to something called Kristen faith and obedience to some god called Krist. Can you imagine that? Hell, that Krist is no Krishna! So what if we can't worship Krishna in the temple, like the others do, he still is our God, ain't he? That Krist, they say, he preached turning the other cheek, being peaceful. Thimma, maybe you so damned ashamed of your caste, I mean your *castelessness*, you become a Kristen or what?"

The pressure was on from both sides. But Thimma was not afraid of his fellow castemen. Or of Marya. He shouted back. "I am no Kristen. I know I am a man from the lowest caste, the casteless caste of society. I accept my condition. Do you?"

Ranga said to Taaya, "Hey, big brother, I think our cousin is really crazy besides being impotent."

Thimma would not be cowed. He said, "You fools! We untouchables have scrubbed and cleaned the bathrooms of all other people as long as India has existed. But today, the greatest person in India, Mahatma Gandhi, cleans our bathrooms; cleans the bathrooms of the untouchables. Who is the greater person, I ask you?"

"Get away from us, you shithead," the brothers shouted.

"No, I am not going to. I am going to stick with you, we are going to stick together, we are going to die together. That's our caste, our destiny. Let me tell you something. A man attains salvation only by being humble. And God has put me, naturally, in that humble state. I am a member of the lowest caste in the world, the casteless caste. I do not have to seek out humility and humiliation so I can find the opportunity to forgive others. I was born with humility and humiliation. I will forgive all, including that poor, pathetic, Police Marya, who spits on me, day after day, because he does not know any better."

"There's nothing pathetic about Marya," said Ranga, the younger cousin. "You are the one who is so *humble* in nourishing your body. You are the one who always talks nonsense; all that cowdung about how 'the soul is the important thing in a human being, not the body, ha, ha, ha!' You don't even eat the pork that we untouchables are allowed to eat with any joy. Look at you. So damned lean and lanky, so thin, your legs resemble those of the village scarecrow."

Taaya joined his brother. There was great frustration in his voice. "Police Marya is not the one who is pathetic," he said. "He is everything you are not. He is no taller than you but there all resemblance stops. He is big. He is heavy-set. He has thick ears, husky lips, a protruding belly. And legs that resemble that of the Master's baby elephant. He's hairy all over and has a shiny head full of deep black hair that is always groomed so rakishly with the Colgate castor oil that he brings from the railway station. He's blacker than coal, shinier than granite. From a distance people mistake him for his cousin, Hanumanth Rao of Badyal. But that Hanumanth Rao, like all of you who praise the Master, like you and like Jimkala Mallanna, has soft, feminine, less wild features. You even have the feminine light-brown color. You are all so damned mild, liking the Brahman Master. But Marya, Marya is the very embodiment, the incarnation of the wild, raffish fierceness that we like."

"And another thing," Ranga added. "He went to school because his father *forced* him to; not because he liked it, *like you!*"

Old man Mallanna had said, "I cannot stand to see *even* untouchables like Sali Thimma go to school and become educated while my son stays home!" And so Marya had trekked to Shamsar Ali's tree-sheltered open-air school near the railway station.

But Marya did not fare too well in school.

Even then he bullied others in class into electing him class leader. "I am at least good in politics," he exclaimed.

Frequently he told his father, the old goat, that the old Muslim teacher needed money. And then he spent the money on chewing-tobacco. By the time he was twelve years old he had enjoyed all varieties of *beedies* and cigarettes available in the village store: *Charminar, Golconda, Panama, Passing Show, Honey Dew* and occasionally even a *Player's Navy Cut.*

On reaching the age of sixteen every one of the boys quit school. The others left for financial and domestic reasons. Marya left in great relief. He was immensely glad he did not have to keep up with the school anymore, for neither did any one his age and generation.

The classmates, Thimma and Marya, both got married at the age of sixteen, as a matter of fact within days of each other. Marya married a subdued, shy, domestic, tiny brown girl from the neighboring village who was a first cousin of Hanumanth Rao of Badyal and second cousin once removed of Jimkala Mallanna.

At seventeen Marya became a father and by the time he was twenty, he had three children.

The old man, the octogenarian goat, kept up with his son. When Marya was twenty-one and about to become the father of a fourth child, he also became, suddenly, an older brother. For at eighty-four, old man Police Mallanna produced a child and went to the village tobacco store to brag about it over a drag of *Passing Show.*

Wild and rakish as he himself was, Marya was slightly embarrassed by his old man's prowess and exuberant fecundity.

The Master, who wanted to heal all wounds and soothe all crinkles of society and history, finally decided to invite Police Marya to his house to join the other three boys from the Muslim's school in the management of the Mansion.

"It's easy for me to give jobs to the other three, boy," he told Police Marya. "But I want to try with you. You are still very young and I am hoping your mind has not been totally poisoned. Maybe you can make a clean break with your family. You know that your father was one of The Sixty who paid to have my father murdered. All his villainy and his goatishness haven't done him much good. I know all this, but I am prepared to forgive and forget. I do not want the sins of the father visited on the son; the sins of The Sixty visited on their progeny. So would you like to work for me, boy?"

Marya was flattered. And pleased. He really had never wanted to be separated from his three schoolmates. He had bullied them; he had acted superior to them; he had even told them that he belonged to some superior caste unknown to mankind. But when separated from the three—from Hanumantha, Jimkala and Thimma—Marya was like a fish out of water. In fact, when, during the first round of discussions, the Master had invited only the other three to the Mansion, Marya had been quite gloomy and violent. He had felt that there was absolutely no chance of his ever going near the Mansion.

Marya knew, of course, of the animosity between his father's family and the Master's. Thus he was quite full of trepidation when the Master invited him to the Mansion. Of course, he didn't tell his father.

But when he returned from the interview, old Police Mallanna was waiting for him. Furious, he locked Marya up in a room full of red pepper.

"What the hell do you mean, you are going to work for that Bomman?" he shouted at the frightened and intimidated Marya. "Don't you know I detest all Bommans, you sonofabitch—the *bitch* that I married, I don't know why? Probably to be punished with the *gift* of such an idiot son! Don't you understand anything? I paid a fortune to get that man's father killed and you want to go serve him? Let me tell you something, buffalo brain! God came to me in a non-Bomman vision once and told me to destroy all Bommans so mankind—India—could be saved. That's why without thinking twice I gave up all my life's savings to the dacoits from the north to destroy that man's father! That man was murdered, thank God for that. But then, like a thousand-headed cobra, this son springs up, that, too, posthumously, as if all the financial efforts of The Sixty made no difference at all! And now *he* carries on as if nothing has changed. I just don't understand God's will! I don't know what else HE wants me to do! I do want to save this country. I did everything in my power to equalize India; to bring the damned, arrogant and powerful Brahman down. And now in the greatest humiliation of my life *you* want to go work for *that* man so he can degrade our caste, again and again."

"That's not the way it was at all, you old goat!" Marya said, becoming quite angry himself. "God damn it, the Master said he wanted to heal all wounds."

"And you believed him? Oh, you buffalo-headed fool! You make the first contact with *that* man and see what happens? You start speaking back to your father; becoming disrespectful and haughty."

Marya was still angry. "I get that from you," he said. He really wanted to do some of what his old classmates were doing.

Old man Mallanna blew his top. "I'll cut your cock off, you damn no-good, lowcaste bastard son of mine, and I'll make it the next eggplant to be offered to Lord Shiva if you ever go near that house again! I'll cut your balls off and plant them as seeds for the tamarind trees for the next generation, you understand! You are going to be the Police Patel of this village! It'll be your job to collect the criminal's tax—the tax that these villagers must pay me so I won't prosecute them as criminals with no regard to whether they have committed a crime or not, the tax that these people pay me so I won't use my power, prosecute them every five days and make life hell for them. You understand? That criminal's tax is our birthright. You will maintain law and order in Kusumurthy when I die. You don't need the Master, boy, don't you know that by now? You are equal to him in every respect. Can your thick buffalo-head grasp that? At least after I die I hope you will grow up and keep tabs on all the people, Bommans, non-Bommans, touchables and untouchables." Here he paused to laugh a minute. "With no inequalities among them. You must treat them all the same, boy," he said, with a knowing wink. "The power, the power comes from you. Not from the Bomman. You are the man of the people. There are more of you than of them. You get my drift, boy?"

3

young goat

THROUGH THIMMA, MARYA SENT an ill-scribbled letter to the Mansion.

Dear Master,
Forgive me, but I must go back on promise. You think
this typical of me as they told you I am always like this
deceitful and unable to keep promise. Sometimes I am but
not with you. I was honored and ready to work for you,
especially, I am not any less than any untouchable, if you
know what I mean, but you know my father how he is, he
is going to cut off my thing if I come to work for you and
you know, sir, that's the most important, the very thing
that I have that makes me superior to all else including
the untouchable, except you, of course, great sir, because I
am sure your mind is as big or bigger than anyone's
thing, you rule over everyone so well, your brain must be
like a big thing. Forgive me for any vulgarity intended.
I promise you, sir, when my father and his thing are dead
and under the earth, I'll come work for you and even if
you know my father was a murderer and even if you
know I've deceived others, I'll be a good servant to you
and a master and manager of all the villagers. I do have a
better brain than the untouchable, dear Master, though no
one believes me.
                            Yours very much in love,
                                    Marya
                                    Police Patel

"Confound the dog," the Master thundered on receiving the
note. "His vulgarity is as repulsive as his father's stupidity!"

Marya drifted apart from the others.
He became a loner, a bully and an outcast from some of the

33

most important transactions that took place in and around Gudur-upon-Bhima. He imitated his father's swagger and his lecherous outlook on life. "I am the young goat of Deccan," he told everyone. Gradually he also developed a considerable knack for borrowing from everyone in the village: the cowdung cleaners, the sweepers, the tree-cutters, the weed-cleaners, the carpenters, the well-diggers, the grave-diggers, the barn-builders, the two widows of the Brahman priest of the Saint's shrine by the river, and the lone barber who owned three sharp razors and the local tobacco shop. Even the distant and stiff Storeman Nagayya was not exempt.

In a short time Marya had accumulated so many debts that people became uncomfortable at asking about repayment. They found it difficult to deal with him. It was both the hopelessness of the task and the intimidation that he practised on them that caused their embarrassment.

The Master's treasurer, Jimkala Mallanna, remarked, "Curious, isn't it, how Marya's delinquency has increased his illegal power in the villages. He threatens everyone. He shouts reprisals at anyone who does not lend him corn or money. In a few years' time he has convinced himself that the various loans given to him are not his debts at all."

When he heard that his own casteman and relative, Jimkala Mallanna, had been critical of him, Marya became quite angry and belligerent. "No wonder my father doesn't like the man named after the disappearing deer," he said. "You cannot be a sissy, like the three, and get anywhere. As the police officer of the village, I am fully entitled to these loans. They are my rights, my 'titles,' let no one be in any doubt. If someone wants protection from his barn being burnt, his store robbed, his well poisoned, his farm sown with weeds, his bullocks injected with buffalo semen, and his hens mated with the barber's geese, he had better forget the repayment of his loans to Police Marya!"

The Master's home minister, his house manager, Hanumanth Rao of Badyal, whose first cousin was married to Police Marya, was quite perturbed.

"My 'brother-in-law' has come to see extortion as his proper function in the villages; as the proper role of the Police Patel," he told Thimma, during one of their many meetings related to the business of the Mansion. "He goes from house to house 'borrowing' from people, the touchables and the untouchables, the people who drink water from the well near the temple and those who drink from the well near the river bend. His notoriety has spread from Kusumurthy to all the neighboring villages. He has come to regard all the villages that lie between the Mansion and the railway station near the Muslim's school as his fiefdom. No one acknowledges his policedom, but no one challenges it openly, either. As usual, word of mouth has done its tremendous work in the Deccan. The law and order man has become the law-and-moral-order problem."

"However, Marya has not touched any of the Master's servants," said Jimkala Mallanna, searching for a glimmer of hope in the situation.

"None except me," thought Thimma. He tried hard to conceal his pain.

But the others were surprised at his evident indifference to the discussion.

They requested the Master to talk to Marya.

The Master summoned Marya again.

"It's your duty to protect your 'wards,'" the Master told Marya diplomatically. "You must protect the people from whom you extort payments. I mean you must protect them from *you.*"

"I don't understand what you are talking about, Master," said Marya, with his usual ability to combine ignorance with mischief.

"When the fence starts grazing the farm, is there any protection left for the crop?" the Master asked Thimma.

"Isn't he wrong, Master? Isn't he really, though? Something must be done against him."

"Thimma! Marya is wrong according to the moral law. But he isn't according to the natural law. The natural law allows power to expand itself like water; to spread as much as the well can contain. Society must react. Society must squeeze him out by standing up to him. Until it does, it must suffer him. Let me tell you an important fact of life. Life is nothing without one's ability to discriminate; to put things in order. One must choose. Most occurrences in life do not necessitate the application of the moral law even though all idealists, in their enthusiasm and their fanaticism, wish to see every event of the world only in moral terms.

They miss the forest for the trees. Excessive use of morality in all matters; continuous use of morality in every little and every big situation; such distinctionless use of morality without hierarchy will sap our vitals; will make us weak when we are most needed. One must discriminate as to when action is warranted and when it's not."

Thimma wondered if the Master knew something he had done that he shouldn't have. He was slightly tense.

The Master continued, smiling slightly at Thimma's discomfiture. "I am not talking about you, Thimma," he said, reassuring the untouchable. "I am speaking in a broad philosophical sense."

Thimma was relieved.

"Of course there comes a time when all issues must cease to be philosophical alone," the Master said. "They must be transformed and polarized so action can be taken. That's the philosophy of *Ramayana* and *Mahabharata*. In both instances the heroes endure suffering for a long time, even renounce kingdoms and exile themselves, so by their example alone they can bring order, justice and harmony to the world. But when that's not possible, Krishna, God, arises to make that necessary and clear distinction between good and evil. And then he exhorts Arjuna to follow the example of *his* previous incarnation, Rama the sea-crosser, and take up arms against a sea of troubles."

"Will this drama have to be played out again and again, father? In the Deccan? In the twentieth century?"

"Forever, my son Thimma, forever. There can be no respite in the world's perpetual illumination. There's so much darkness that needs to be dealt with. Nature recognizes good and evil and places them in its picture like two color blots that envelop one another, depending upon the time, the circumstance and the will of the people involved. Only the philosopher sees all evil in himself and all possibilities for good in the world. He does not understand, or refuses to accept, the true and proper distinction between good and evil and their natural ability to keep each other in check and balance. But! But the philosopher's despair need not be *our* despair in regard to Marya."

"Master! Are you suggesting that he who has the rod has the buffalo?"

"Only until the man with the bigger rod, the divine rod, appears on the scene."

"Where's the limit, father? When can we consider that Marya has crossed the boundary?"

"When he invades your bed. Or puts a knife to your throat."

"And then you will intervene?"

"Someone will. The first responsibility to triumph over evil, to confront and to conquer it, must lie with the individual. When the misery becomes universal, the complaint must be registered."

Little Rangi—his, hers and that dark shiny fat black man's —strolled onto the porch and made faces at him.

She was a miniature of her mother, Ganga, whom he had loved so much once and whom now he hated with passionate, lustful, incurable jealousy.

4

beautiful woman

THIMMA REMEMBERED THE THORN trees. Sparse as they were by the river bend, they were sufficient to conceal the married couple who wanted to behave like lovers. Thimma had wanted her since the day he set his eyes on her at the pre-engagement bridal interview. She was tall and fair and had beautiful black hair, eyes like those of a deer (the eyes had deceived him, O Heron!), lips lush and curved as those of a goddess in a Hindu temple that he could only see and not touch, and legs tall and straight as sugarcane at harvest time.

Even among untouchables, who were the outcastes of India, Indian customs were strictly followed. If they went for a walk the wife always had to follow the man, at a distance. Seven days after his marriage, his father, Rama, and his mother, Nandini, had given him permission to go out with his wife for a walk to the river.

Thimma delighted in the walk. He was free, excited, dreamy, full of poetic passion. Always a beautiful singer, Thimma sang wonderfully all the way to the river. The flat, infinite Deccan seemed to absorb his beautiful song in its forever-moving-on, hot, dry winds.

So did Ganga.

The wind rustled her. With her crimson red wedding mark on her forehead glowing like a little, unreal moon, her red-and-black checkered saree demurely covering her head of flowing black hair, little silver ringlets gracing her naked feet, she followed her man and his song with tremendous anticipation.

She knew what would happen when they got to the river. She wanted it. Him. In his slim, intense, poetic way Thimma was handsome and desirable, wasn't he? She felt herself rebelling against her family already. For the first time in seven days, Thimma and she would be totally alone this afternoon, something they could never be in that joint family full of great-uncles and great-aunts, brothers-in-law who were really Thimma's first and second cousins, father-in-law and mother-in-law.

The rocks had been rendered smooth by the river. The sun shone bright, energetic and pitiless. Water bouncing over the boulders glistened. Thimma laid his back against the smooth orange rock halfway down the river's breadth. He held Ganga against the rock. As he entered her, he hugged her firm, smooth buttocks underneath her checkered red-and-black saree. Ganga was as smooth and firm and challenging as the orange rock behind him, the rock that was an example of what stones became when touched by the river. Between the Deccan stone and the Deccan woman, both smooth and hard at the same time, was ecstasy.

The glistening river made him think of his future. For the schoolman-untouchable who had recently been appointed the Master's "son," and who had married the most beautiful untouchable woman in the countryside, the future looked as beautiful as the wife who was sucking him so gently now.

O Ganga!

In seven days of anticipation and excitement and mutual discovery; in seven days of marriage, how close they had become!

"Our parents did know us well, didn't they?" Thimma said.

Ganga said, "Maybe, in some ways, they knew us better than we ourselves did."

"That's why they arranged this marriage, which must have been made in heaven." Thimma looked at Ganga again. She blushed crimson.

"In the Deccan there is much to be grateful for."

"Good parents are one of those things."

"In Deccan marriage comes first and then love follows inevitably, Ganga. As night follows day."

"Let us spread our rumals here," Thimma's friend, Jimkala "Disappearing Deer" Mallanna, said, staring at the sunset.

"I'd rather be away from the thorn trees," Thimma said, looking for a refuge in the river rocks. Finally, they found two massive, beautiful rocks.

"Have a *beedi.*"

"You better not be seen sharing a smoke with an untouchable."

"There is no one here but the river."

They laughed genially. Thimma smoked. He stared at the horizon across the river. Ganga's village was there.

"Why did your cousins want the most beautiful untouchable girl in the Deccan to marry you?" Jimkala asked.

"Because they had heard the notoriously well-publicized news that for the first time in the history of the Deccan, an untouchable had been appointed the 'son' of the Master. And they wanted to be joined to the Master's family. Her father, the mustachiod matchmaker, said, 'The Master is the most distinguished, the most powerful and the most feared man in this area encircled by the three Deccan rivers Bhima, Krishna and Tungabhadra. We all know he has intimate connections with the most important person in India —Mahatma Gandhi.' "

"Then how come they haven't approached you for any favors from the Master?"

"Because two years after my marriage to Ganga, the missionaries came, and then the whole village of six hundred people, including all of her cousins and brothers and parents, became Kristens."

"Did that bother you?"

"I did not mind what they did as much as why they did it. The missionaries had offered them money and transistor radios and beds and jewels and battery-operated chopping knives."

"Well, well! Battery-operated chopping knives!"

"I knew then that my relatives had offered their daughter to me for the same reason that they had offered themselves to the missionaries—in the hope of power, position and influence by association in return for their daughter."

"Aren't you being a little harsh?" Jimkala said, soothing Thimma.

"The fact is I don't mind having Kristen cousins. After all, I had always believed that Hindus and Kristens were cousins— children of the same God—and now this belief has become reality. It is the taunts of my people in Kusumurthy that exasperate me. Cousin Taaya, who is already upset about my joining the Master's household, is now completely in a flame about my in-laws' conversion. 'Not only is that bastard Thimma a sissy,' he shouts, 'but to insult *me* further he has married into a family of bastard believers, Indian Christians; people who are neither men nor women.' "

"What's on your mind, boy?" the Master asked Thimma.

"My in-laws becoming Kristens, Master."

"Why not, boy?" the Master asked him, sitting peacefully on a simple Kinwat carpet outside the village temple. The temple was the local Hindu shrine. "Why do you taunt your poor wife's cousins for becoming Christians? We haven't done any better by them. We have taken every bit of religion and made it stand on its head. We have caused the unholy mixture of philosophy and sociology for more than a thousand years now and we have claimed, quite mendaciously, that God, our Hindu God, wanted it this way. Does this God inside this temple want it this way? You really think so? Answer me, boy! I hear some people are doing the same thing in the West. Some pseudo-philosophers there are claiming that racism is nothing but God-given casteism, that the whites are Brahmans and the blacks are untouchables, and the amazing part of it all is that some of them are claiming sanction for their theories in our scriptures as well as their Bible. Some German idiot claims that the swastika, the most auspicious symbol of peace and prosperity in our three-thousand-year-old home, is his own. Well, what can I say! Well! If these missionaries are not *those* Bible people and if they accept your cousins, the untouchables of India, as equals under God, let your cousins become Christians, I say! Go and become one too, son! Maybe that'll be good for you. Open more doors!"

"No, I'll never do that, Master. I will not forsake our traditions, our society, our life—what has made this country go on for so long."

"You mean what has caused this country's prolonged agony? I hope you don't expect me to be grateful to you for not converting?"

"No, Master, no! Heaven forbid. Why should you be grateful? This is my karma. By good deeds and by good thoughts, by loyalty and courage and intelligence, I expect to live the best life I possibly can within the limits God has assigned me. And then, in the next incarnation, I will transcend my condition. I assure you I will. I will progress one step at a time, as each lifetime passes by."

"Oh, my, my! Your optimism is quite fantastic! And I must say quite transcendental! You are better than all the thousand Brahmans—priests and laymen alike—with whom I eat and discourse and conduct marital discussions. You are like the Saint Kanakadasa, the untouchable who pleased Krishna more than all the Brahmans. If you believe in the caste system you'll have to wait a thousand years before you are redeemed. We are still in the second half of Kali Yuga, the period of sin and deprivation. Our racism and our caste system and our desire to oppress our brothers, all that appears so inevitable to us, are only manifestations of the quality of the time we live in. Maybe in a thousand years the new world will dawn on us, but that we don't know. Some years ago I was in England, and at an idyllic place called Oxford, a poet told me that even the second coming of their God—their Christ—was uncertain. We can't wait forever, son! The world is changing faster than the systems within it.

"Are you sure you did not misunderstand this missionary of yours? Prejudge him?"

Thimma stared at the Master sitting on the carpet on the stone seat high above him. He stared at the temple behind the Master.

"No, father! He came across clear as a Hindu temple bell I can hear but cannot ring. Since that day, I let Ganga visit her people any time she wants to, but I never go to see them."

"Did Ganga become a Christian before she married you?"

"No, Master. This happened two years after we were married."

"Are you taking good care of that young girl, boy? She's too pretty for you and your ambitions. Don't, and I say again, don't ever neglect your conjugal duties. Otherwise she'll bring you certain ruin."

"What do you mean, Master?"

"In the Deccan an empty bed at night means a tragic home by day. These Deccan girls! Your mistress, my wife, is one of them. Their passion is surpassed only by their sense of possession. Be very careful, boy! Don't neglect Ganga! Or else she will cause a havoc."

"Yes, Master! My friend! My father!"

The great Hindu festival, Deepavali, was in full swing at the Mansion. Parapets and cupolas were decorated with earthenware lamps. Several people were dining in different rooms. Sparkling lights swirled in the inner courtyard and the huge outside compound, and firecrackers exploded everywhere.

Thimma was thinking of converting to Buddhism. Only a few weeks before, in a Deccan city called Aurangabad—not too far away from Ajanta and Ellora, the cave temples that had been created by the munificence of the Buddhist monarchs of the Deccan and the aesthetic powers of the Buddhist monk-artists of the Deep South—a man named Ambedkar had organized a mass conversion of the untouchables to Buddhism.

"Ambedkar has organized a mass conversion of the untouchables to Buddhism, sir," Thimma said, trying to catch the Master's attention.

"Ambedkar the untouchable is a genius," the Master exclaimed. "He has risen to become the law minister of India and one of the fathers of our constitution."

"I am very much inspired by him, Master. But I cannot, for the life of me, understand why the great Buddha's religion has not taken deep roots in India, particularly in our part of India, in our Deccan, when it is rumored to have spread all over China and Japan. Can this neo-Buddhism, Ambedkar's neo-Buddhism, survive and establish itself and transform India?"

The Master himself started thinking about Buddha's life in Nepal and Bihar and later, as Thimma continued to wonder about Buddhism. "No, it does not seem to be for me," he thought. We Indians are too much people of this world to believe in absolute self-denial.

"I cannot do it, sir," he told the Master, who was busy playing with a firecracker, like a child, and entertaining his children. "Like all Hindus I believe very much in the physical and material world; in the power and glory of it."

"Okay," said the Master and turned to his son. "Vishnoo, get away from the fire. It might explode in your face, boy. Get away. Even in a great festival there is great danger."

"Me, not afraid, father," said little Vishnoo, as he boldly put his hand on top of the bright white sparkler streaming forth.

"Get away, son," said the Master, lifting the child in his arms.

Thimma had to tell the Master why he could not convert to

Buddhism, even when the most famous untouchable in India had done it. "I want to understand the intricacies of Indian society and I want to master them, sir!" he told the Master, who was now busy giving orders for the arrangement of the great evening meal. "I believe in buying and selling and borrowing and lending. I even enjoy—if I can use that word to describe my feeling—the complex and subtle power play that goes on in this countryside endlessly."

"And in those chess games you are always able to win, outsmarting the upper-caste people," the Master interrupted him. Thimma was surprised to hear the Master respond to him. For a while he had thought the Master was not paying a bit of attention.

"The power lies in your mind, boy, I know. You have touched power and you cannot give it up."

Whenever the exercise of influence and of lending rights caused conflict between his Master and the newly emerging landlords from the middle castes, Thimma was always the troubleshooter. That's what the late night meetings were all about. The others always lost out to him, first because they were confounded that a Brahman would trust an untouchable over themselves, and then because Thimma, the cunning untouchable, always knew his facts and figures better than they did.

There was also one other very important reason for thinking he could never convert to ascetic Buddhism. He would never be able to practice abstinence and self-denial with his beautiful, erotic, Hindu-goddess-like wife.

5

village robbed

O N A BLEAK DECEMBER DECCAN evening when the sun set too early and disappeared in the shallow waters of the rocky river, when dusk began to settle down, Thimma returned from the rice fields to watch a spectre in his house. Surprise had been his as he saw his tall, slender, ivory-white wife, adorned with wild daisies in her dark jet-black hair—all interwoven, those wild daisies, into one entangled spider's web, by the long, thin, imitation silver brooch he had bought her from the meager peanut crop of last summer—with a red necklace and a checkered red blouse, and a blue handloomed saree from Sholapur covering only her thighs and exposing her slender sinuous legs; and a monumental belly moving up and down under the blue coarse shirt, the brown-white dhoti flipped half-open like that of the woman, his—Thimma's— wife under *him;* and he, Sali Thimma, the man who went to school, the man who was a product of the Deccan villages, the man who had outgrown the country superstitions of seeing ghosts at dusk by the riverside, wished again that what he saw at a banyan tree's distance away from him were only a ghost. But the wish failed to deceive him. He knew that the man and his hulking, lascivious and lusty body could be identified even at dusk. It was his old school-mate Police Marya.

Standing under the banyan tree, looking at the porch of his own house, Thimma contemplated his own body. Light brown. Half the size of the man who was on top of his wife. Arms and legs worn thin by the drudgery of keeping himself alive and dignified; legs worn with the effort of supporting his family, of walking miles and miles behind the Master's bullock cart to the nearby railway station; hands bruised by trying to build fences around his haystack (for while he was his Master's "son" he was *his* own only servant and all care for his personal property had to come from him); eyes sunken with the pain of wanting to see everything; cheeks hollowed

45

by sacrifice of his own food for his children during the years that lacked monsoon; clothed by a ragged, colorless shirt, a brown dhoti that became fresher or dirtier as he washed it or did not wash it in the muddy stream near his father's grave; and a one-and-only turban that covered the mass of his hair. All his money went to buy and to farm the land; every drop of money went into the little property like drops of his blood.

Sali Thimma compared himself with the man there—rich, extravagant, a spendthrift with a huge, monumental ass. Deep inside, he realized, he—Thimma—was a coward. If he tried to confront the two, they would mock him, jeer at his lack of "manliness." The wife might even crack a cruel joke about his virility. He felt very lonely. He dared not enter his own house. He wondered where his two older sons were and when they would be back. Scalding tears burned his sunbrowned cheeks. Loosening his turban he wiped his face. He felt like a child. He needed to be consoled.

Slowly, reflecting, he walked on in the transcendent dusk, over the sandy little footpath beyond all the trees of the village path, to the bare levee, shaven of grass and pasture, and headed in the direction of the village that once used to be.

Thirty years ago everyone had moved away from the village that once was; the village called Kalla Halli, or the Village Robbed.

The most enterprising ones went to Bombay, ticketless travelers on express trains to that milling island of desperation 400 miles away. The less enterprising ones went to Sholapur, the cottonmill capital of the Southwest 200 miles away, to live in the comfort of electricity, movie houses and a watertap that brought water to them, one hour a day. Sholapur! That cotton-mill city from whose factories had come the saree, clad in which his wife was giving herself away to that black elephant. What a symbol of infidelity cotton mills had become to him!

Some others went to nearby Yadgir forty miles away to work as porters at the railway station, as stonebreakers at the huge blasted mountain, or as bathroom cleaners at the local missionary hospital for forty paise a day. They left their ill-constructed houses, their mud barns and their thatched huts, and they migrated.

So did Thimma and Thimma's father thirty years ago. Only they went away not to Bombay or Sholapur or Yadgir, but to Kusumurthy, the village that was four miles away, the village whose name meant "a Child's Image."

When his father, Rama, had died, twenty years ago, Thimma had brought him back to the grounds of the ghost village, "the Village Robbed," Kalla Halli, the lonely place. Brought him to one of the Master's fields and buried him not too far from the abandoned village temple of Hanuman, the temple that still stood implacably in the midst of the total desolation surrounding it, as if it were a symbol of the perpetuity and continuity of Indian civilization in the midst of all its material destitution. The temple built of smooth Bhima rocks was a shrine dedicated to the Deccan god, Hanuman, the god of monkeys, who was supposed to have built the bridge to cross the Indian Ocean from Cape Comorin to Ceylon, two thousand five hundred years ago.

Night gathered.

Night enveloped Thimma's consciousness. Gradually, memories of his life, his past—his youth in Kalla Halli, the Village Robbed; his life decimated by his people's migration—flickered away, lighting up for brief moments and then becoming nothing, like the starflies of the Deccan evenings, making continuing whirring noises, chirpy eerie rhythms, no music around, evocative, emerging out of the coming darkness of his life. The vast, dry, brown land, cropless, houseless, peopleless, the land to which he had stuck with such interminable tenacity, the land of a father who was long dead and gone, struck him as fearful now. In the wilderness of confused emotions, Thimma looked up at the sky above him —at the stars—hoping it would rain.

In Kalla Halli, in that Village Robbed, in that now never-never land of his adolescence when he and his father used to come to this now beghosted field, in coarse woolen blankets made into hooded covers for themselves to guard the field and the harvest, the coming of rain was always a moment of bliss. It washed away all problems. Or it had then.

It rained now. But Thimma—peasant, village leader of all the 125 untouchables, the leader of the last caste in India, the untouchables, the people whom Gandhi had called the children of God; the man who had always tried to rule his unruly, ax-wielding, violent-tempered cousins and uncles, who always got into a fight with the people of the upper castes; the man who was respected, feared and secretly despised by all the people of the village for his intelligence and his cunning in solving all problems under the banyan tree; the man who had always thwarted and frustrated the village people's ambitions to kill each other; the man who had loved the land; the man who had throbbed to the occasional music of the Deccan; that man was cold and hostile. He wanted revenge. He hated the fact of his having been away, night after night, in sun, in rain and in cold, away, taking care of his Brahman Master's house, its accounts and its affairs, to further his ambition and the pride of his caste.

To further his ambition and the pride of his caste he had given up his bed, his family, his life, his sense of honor. Had he not become the first man from his caste who had risen to the position of the "son" of the Gudur estate, an estate owned for two thousand years and more by ruling Brahmans? The Master of the estate, the owner of the mango orchard, had respected him since he was a little boy, a brave young man of only sixteen. Since that day of recognition, every day had meant the rise of his star, higher and higher. And then for his wife, Ganga, and his family, he had disappeared into the higher and invisible galaxies of ruling power.

But to gain that position, to show uncompromising intelligence and indefatigable and unceasing loyalty, he had had to make many, many sacrifices.

Always work came first. So fascinated had Thimma been by the eros of intelligence and power that the mere sensuality of sleeping with his cheaply bejewelled wife had seemed mediocre; little more than a chore. Thimma had tried to establish himself not only as the most intelligent but also as the most moral man in the Deccan villages. Thus he had touched no other woman in his life except his wife; and that too he had done out of what he thought was sheer necessity; more as a moral responsibility that he owed to Ganga and to his dead father, who had united them in holy wedlock.

For ten years there was not a single deal made; not a single farm sold; a single tree cut in the area; a single wedding held; without Thimma knowing about it. In sheer frustration, Police Marya exclaimed: "The village bull will not burp, the village whore will not have her evening client and the village teacher will not take on a new student, without finding out from that untouchable if it's the right thing to do." His Master, his true father, the Brahman prince-farmer, had told him that though he was a Harijan by birth, he was a Brahman by intelligence: hence the title given to him had stuck to him like a mark of adultery. Sali Thimma meant School-man Thimma.

He wished his father, Rama, were alive to see how high a human being, and that too the son of an untouchable, could go in the pursuit of excellence and nobility—yes, nobility. For with his acquired power Thimma had done nothing except what the most ambitious people in the world have always wanted to do—to solve all disputes by peace, in peace—be peacemakers and be known for it.

But tonight, amid the continuing flicker and the whirring sound of the strange Deccan insects, the desire for peace seemed to be disappearing under the cold rain. The ardent moral fervor on which he had built his life seemed to be quenched. The great Indian epics of *Ramayana* and *Mahabharata*, the stories of battle and sacrifice that he had read with such passion, intelligence and care, the melodic tender songs of the great poets of the Kannada language that he had known so well, offered no solace to him. But the melancholy folk song that his grandmother and her sister used to sing while pounding corn into flour, the song whose lines said,

> With the speed of time and
> The need of the swift bird,
> She left him for the scarecrow
> And the lark was no more the bird.

those crazy lines haunted him,

Thimma sat by his father's grave in the middle of the peanut farm.

Forgiveness on his part would not be recognized by his wife or her paramour. They had cuckolded him to the village and declared him to be a man who had sent his essence to his head. But Thimma wanted them to recognize him, to know that he was right and they were wrong, that he was still the most intelligent man in the countryside, and that they had done something wrong —quite unintelligent. He wondered if his father could help him, if there was indeed another world, and if some message would be forthcoming from the other world of honorable men—his dead father's and his live, father-like Master's.

And the educated man hypersensated by defeat and anguish saw his father, with the little goat, walking in the distance, the old man's clean turban, the sparkling cunning eyes, the tall, lanky body all compact even after death, even while he, Thimma, was sitting right next to the solitary grave of the man who was walking towards him. This was the ghost village, Kalla Halli, the Village Robbed.

Thimma wanted to believe in this vision as much as he wanted to believe that what he had seen in the verandah of his own house, this evening, had been a vision.

His father came near him. Thimma saw him very clearly. The old man looked very much like him. He appeared the same age as Thimma was. He appeared the same age at which he, Rama, had died.

Confusion and timorousness grasped Thimma's imagination. He shuddered at his father—now his own age—coming at him. He also shuddered at the thought of the imminent disappearance of the vision.

"Please don't," he shouted loudly to himself, wanting to run away, yet remaining paralyzed.

Thimma's father laughed wildly. Thimma wanted to concentrate his whole past of twenty, thirty years into an instant and tell the old man what a good and worthy son he had been, almost beg his father not to chide him, prove himself in front of the old man, prove that he had done right—and even better than that—by the family.

Gradually but decidedly, the apparition became more wild and more threatening. It thundered. It deafened him.

Still he could hear the distant rumble of the river. The river and the temple always remained. He could see the vast, lonely, dark countryside.

The goat bleated in a crazy discord, punctuating and orchestrating the dead old man's hysteria.

"O you intelligent fool! Why did you try to gain the world and lose the hearth? Why? How could that big, black fat man take your wife? The wife to whom you have been so loyal, faithful? I want no reconciliation. I want revenge. And you do too. Nothing else will satisfy me. Or you!"

Thimma perspired. He did not want to stay on the farm. Or in Kalla Halli, the Village Robbed, the ghost village. He wanted to run away from there.

There was no place to run to except back to the place of his humiliation, his own house. He must seek answers amid reality. He must set things right. He must not seek advice from his father. Once again he must be better than his father and find the solution to his problem on his own.

The hysterical laughter and the crazy bleating deafened his senses. He ran.

Away from Kalla Halli, the ghost village of his youth, his past, Thimma hurried back to the village of his tenebrous present, Kusumurthy, the village named after the child's image. He needed to find consolation in the midst of the cause of his grief.

Dark night gathered the desolate barren land in its sightless nothingness. The lonely middle-aged man, returning from his village of memories, wanted human company that would comfort him.

Thimma climbed the guard tower of the wet paddy fields. In the distance he could see the flicker of a lamp swaying.

6

countryside in modern times

THE LAMPS WERE TURNED OFF at the Mansion. The Master and his family had gone to sleep.

Hanumantha Rao of Badyal and Thimma gathered at the outside office of the Mansion that was an elementary school in daytime. It was for their periodic nightly session of rambling discussion. They were both chronic insomniacs, a professional hazard of working in important positions at the Mansion.

"You know that you are quite capable of evil, Thimma!" Hanumantha Rao of Badyal said. "Schooling has not taught you the means to be above yourself."

"What do you mean?"

"I know, Thimma. You have skimmed off the Master. Every time the Master sends you to mediate a loan repayment, you come back and inform the Master that the debtor has agreed to pay only half the amount due on the condition that his account is cleared and he is absolved of any future obligations."

"True."

"What you don't bother to tell is that in actuality, you have collected not half but seventy-five percent of the debt."

"You think the Master knows?"

"Is the Deccan a poor land?"

"Ninety percent of the debts in the villages are bad debts," said Thimma. "It is a wonder we can collect anything at all. The peasants complain eternally of bad harvest, bad weather and bad luck. All of this in their case is true. The land—having provided sustenance to the Dravidians, the Aryans, the Huns, the Badamis, the Hoysalas, the Golconda kings, the Moghul emperors, the Marathas, the Nizams and all their vassal princes and their many subjects—the land tilled for more than four thousand years now is tapped out. It needs an enormous, heroic and superhuman, and perhaps super-Indian, effort to be improved. There is no such

effort. There can be none. Most people's efforts are concentrated
on earning one meal a day. The Master's resources, though enormous by the peasants' standards, go mainly into the maintenance
of this 3,000 year-old house that was built before the Aryans came
to the Indus valley. There is the maintenance of the stables, the
wages of his workers, and the lending out to all the needy ones in
the countryside, even when he knows beforehand that ninety percent of his debts will never be paid back."

"Perhaps that's why he appreciates you. Quietly ignores your
skimming. He knows how hard it is to get anything back. Let's go
and see what our tadi man is doing. Maybe a few drinks tonight?"

"Why not?"

They reached the bamboo shop. Hanumantha Rao of Badyal
made himself comfortable on the bench. Thimma sat on the ground.
Tadi was served. There was no one else in the shop.

They drank the tadi. Thimma said, "In thirty-six years of his
rule, the Master has not saved a thousand rupees. But hundreds of
families, occasionally importuning him, occasionally deceiving
him, have lived their lives, eating cornbread three times a day—
cornbread that is occasionally garnished with butter or peanut oil
or red pepper by the vegetarian merchant castes, chicken by your
middle-caste families, and pig by my untouchables."

Hanumantha Rao of Badyal was fully drunk. "I wonder if
hope will ever come to our scorched earth."

Thimma's eyes moistened.

The Master was seated on the high stoneseat in the outer
courtyard facing the artesian well. Thimma was seated on the
ground. The evening train to Hyderabad was visible in the far
distance. The Master shared the Sunday paper with Thimma.

"The money Americans are pouring into India!" the Master
said to Thimma, glancing at the newspaper.

"Neither of us has seen any of it, sir," Thimma said, laughing
gently.

"Come here, boy. Look. Pictures of farms in the state of
Punjab."

"There grain stands taller than the farmers, who are themselves quite tall," Thimma said. "We Deccaners are short people, Master."

"The caption says: 'Model Farm Near the Nation's Capital.' "

"The Deccan is very far from New Delhi, Master. The Deccan is absolutely in the middle of nowhere. Nothing ever happens here. The Arabian Sea is 300 miles away, the Bay of Bengal is equally far, the Indian Ocean even farther. And the Himalayas? The source of so much water in India? The Himalayas are even farther than New Delhi."

"But let us not forget the river, boy. The river Bhima is everything. The river Bhima is full of rocks, beautiful and dangerous orange rocks, white and pink and clean black rocks, asphalt grey rocks, rocks that have made the Deccan famous, rocks that have gone into the construction of the world-famous Golconda fort that is in itself a huge rock, full of apertures but no exit."

Late afternoon they went to the river, Thimma ten steps ahead of the Master, as always.

The Master sat in the river sand that was burying Shiva's temple. Thimma sat slightly away, yet within a listening distance.

Today, by Shiva's temple, the Master was wondering about America.

"What a grand place it must be," he said. "A miracle caused by rain and man and God acting in perfect harmony. The soil of America. How virgin and fecund it must be. Not blighted by the drain of civilization!"

The Master listened to the rhythms of the river. The Master dreamed of Kansas and Iowa and Nebraska, of exotic places such as Milwaukee and Minneapolis and St. Louis and Memphis and New Orleans. Billions of wheat grains flew up to the skies like birds, and blinded the earth and heavens.

The potatoes of Idaho lay buried in zillions in a farm full of snow and prosperity that resembled a hefty, underground, globular paradise, holding within it all the prosperous hemispheres.

"Thimma!"

"Yes, sir?"

"I want to graft the whole virgin, beautiful, rich land of America with the barren, dry, woe-ridden earth of my scorched Deccan. Ah! How does one make a new beginning in such an old land? I am myself merely fulfilling my cardinal Hindu responsibility of not neglecting the ones I live with, those in my present; never neglecting the living present, until it is ready to expire."

"Why, Master, anything is possible in this modern world of ours!"

"Is it? I surely hope so, boy. Perhaps Vishnoo will go to America someday. Perhaps. Perhaps he will get himself an education into the future. I hope he will plan and dream and act. I hope he will marry an idealistic American girl, some girl with an age-old and simple name like Margaret! Americans are always so full of idealism, Thimma! They are the only people in the whole history of human civilization that have the audacity to attempt to make human life better. And they have almost succeeded. They are after something called the pursuit of happiness. Such an un-Indian thing isn't it, this pursuit of happiness! We are not comfortable unless we are miserable. That's the Old World for you. I hope the little Prince, my Vishnoo, will bring his American bride back to Gudur-upon-Bhima. I hope he will unite these two lands. The first European thought he was looking for India when he found America. I have read a lot about their thinkers who have been influenced by us. We certainly have been influenced by them."

Suddenly, the Master became rueful, almost melancholic. "But I don't know if it will happen, Thimma," he said. "Not in my lifetime anyway. The task is so enormous."

Vishnoo, the little Prince, had a lot going for him.

As a child he had impressed the Deccaners as observant and alert and very much a companion to his father. The culture and sense of history of the old Master seemed to have rubbed off considerably on the young man. Vishnoo was admitted to a primary school in Hyderabad at age three and within six months he was so far ahead of the other children that the Headmaster gave him a double promotion to the third grade. In the third grade the little Prince learned to recite the difficult Urdu poetry with great finesse.

Vishnoo liked challenges. He learned mathematics; English; and the history of the Deccan.

Growing up in Hyderabad part of the time and in the country-side part of the time, the Prince wondered often about his father's favorite person, Thimma.

In the countryside, whenever possible, the Prince coaxed Thimma to go with him to Shiva's temple by the river.

"The river always brings me back, Thimma. The river, I love this river."

"Yes, little Master. It has purified us more than once."

"Thimma, you and I are named after the same God. We are both *sons* of the Master. We both like the same things; poetry, history, mathematics. But you can never be called Vishnoo because you are an untouchable. And I can never be called Thimma because I am a Brahman. Something needs to be done about that."

"That's inviting great trouble, little Master. You must learn from your father. Change. But pay attention to the difficulties."

"I don't care about difficulties. I am tired of difficulties. Quite impatient with them. I want change. Anyway, what did Father mean by saying you and I are two different aspects of the same being; two sides of the same coin?"

"I don't know, Master. But he does dream about you a lot. He hopes you will be able to go to America some day."

"I also dream of things for the Deccan, Thimma, yes, I do. If I go to America I will live near the coast of New Jersey or the coast of California so I can take off and return to Gudur-upon-Bhima at the shortest notice. The thought of going to America makes me lonely, Thimma."

"Why, little Master?"

"I wonder if I will be lonely and lost in America without my people. I hope I will have a definite purpose in going to America. I want to be a leader."

"But you are."

"No, not in the usual way. But a thinker; a writer. I want to come back and improve the land. Arrange for hundreds of tractors to till the land—my father's, yours.' "

"They are your lands too, young Prince."

"Yes, but only in trust. I want to build several waterways. Set up irrigation pumps attached to the river Bhima and to all the wells in the countryside. Those by Hanuman's temple and those by the

riverbend. For the upper castes and the untouchables. I am going
to construct a modern road from the railway station to the Mansion.
I will build a road from Krishna-upon-Bhima to Gudur-upon-
Bhima. I will build culverts over ditches (including the one in which
Grandfather's head was concealed for ten days after his murder)
and streams. I will even out the surface of this Deccan earth!"

"It is a beautiful dream, little Master."

Vishnoo was perfectly inspired by Thimma's company.
Thimma brought out the best in him. "I will build five well-stocked,
well-lighted library-cum-schools in the five villages. I will build a
house exactly at the center of the area of Gudur-upon-Bhima, which
would fall just outside the borders of Kusumurthy, the village of
the untouchables, for me, because the most important untouchable
lives there. My house will be a modern house with thirty-two rooms,
electricity, water supply, and a beautiful verandah overlooking the
river, where father and mother can host moonlight dinners for their
closest friends—Hanumanth Rao of Badyal, Jimkala Mallanna, the
old Muslim from Raichur, Allah Baksh and you. I will improve
your lot and build you a nice house not too far from my own, so
we could be within calling distance of each other."

"Thank you, Master. Let us go back to the Mansion now. Or
else mother will be worried."

Many times Vishnoo had wanted to touch Thimma's feet because Thimma was so intelligent and so humble. The little Prince
wanted to be humble in front of the humble man.

Every time the Prince had come near Thimma, Thimma had
run away or hidden where he could. The Prince's mother told him
sternly, "You are being really cruel to Thimma! You are making
his life miserable by not respecting the rules of society."

One day the little Prince touched Thimma anyway. He had to
go back and take a big hot bath in the huge inner bathroom with
skylights. He had to cleanse himself.

Sometimes, when the Prince visited the countryside, Thimma
was unavailable, having gone off on one of his many errands.

"Life is miserable here without Thimma," he told his mother.
"I can discuss almost anything with him. He knows what the proper

thing is. He knows who should accompany me where, when and why. He knows what houses I should 'grace' by my visit. His house is not one of them."

His mother said, "I am glad he makes sure you never offend your father by breaking the rules of hierarchy and propriety. When he is around you I don't worry as much. I don't feel so bad about your father being always busy, highly involved as he is in national legal and political matters, as long as Thimma is somewhere arou 1d. You have learned from him where to give your audience, the proper uses of the *Diwan-e-Khas* and *Diwan-e-Aam.*"

One adjourned to the *Diwan-e-Khas* for people who mattered. For ceremonial audiences of goodwill, one proceeded to the *Diwan-e-Aam* overlooking the river. For very private or potentially scandalous matters, one had to take refuge in the inner courtyard of Shahabad marble. And in some even more extreme and potentially explosive cases, the negotiations had to be moved to the second-floor East Bedroom.

"Your father says Thimma briefs you in advance on all discussions with neighboring landlords and loan sharks."

"Yes, mother. He protects the Mansion's interests with well-researched, advance information. Above all, he has shown me that the Mansion's interests and the interests of the Deccan are one and the same. Above all, mother, he dreams with me. That's the bond between us."

When the Master and the Prince were at the Mansion at the same time, such as during summer vacations, the Master, the Prince and Thimma took many morning walks to the fields, soon after their traditional early morning tea, to supervise the agriculture and to talk about the future.

Part Two

7

master

Early morning, the cool breeze came over the Bhima river.
The landscape was sparsely dotted with lonely trees that
marked boundaries between two farms—two desolate pieces
of earth.

The Master knew that once the land had been full of trees and
orchards of grapes and mangoes, for which the soil had always been
receptive. But with the arrival of modern times; with everyone's
desire to do things faster than before; with the gradual decimation
and the ultimate loss of the great Oriental quality of patience,
superhuman and unreal, the Master had to move to the great center
of Deccan, to the metròpolis—the elegant city of Hyderabad.

In Hyderabad, he was to get himself a brilliant education, stay
always at the top of his class, and win every scholarship that was
ever instituted at the fledgling Osmania University. Then came law,
political imprisonment for radical work under the Mahatma, and
defense of fellow revolutionaries whenever he himself was let out
of jail on brief furloughs. Finally came the independence of India
and the offers by Nehru of ambassadorships to China or the Soviet
Union or Great Britain—or any place in the world that he wanted
to go.

But he had not wanted to go any place other than his ancestral
home—the old Mansion full of history and uncomfortable invita-
tions. So, as a compromise, came acceptance of a judgeship on the
Supreme Court of India. But his crazy notion of wanting to conduct
the Supreme Court of India in all the nooks and corners of the
country, in hamlets and lonely hills, became more and more unac-
ceptable to his fellows on the bench and to the government in New
Delhi. His theory, Gandhian and quixotic, was that since eighty-
three percent of India's people lived in the villages, he, represent-
ing their aspirations, should live with them. Indian justice should
emanate from a "courtroom" in a thatched hut, or from an old

ruined temple, rather than from the British-constructed, elaborate and ornate Greek-Victorian court buildings in New Delhi. Because of their economic, social and administrative concerns, his fellow judges and the Central Government opposed his Gandhian "back-to-the-village" movement. They created insurmountable difficulties for him. The Indian politicians and their henchmen-masters, the Indian bureaucrats, were past-masters at creating petty and unbearable problems. Still, whenever he was the one to adjudicate a case singly or to hear a petition without colleagues, he conducted hearings in a remote hamlet in the state of Manipur on the Burmese border; in the camel-ridden sands of Rajasthan bordering scorched West Pakistan; in the island villages of Laccadive in the Indian Ocean; and in the little village of Gudur-upon-Bhima where he was born.

Finally they issued an executive order and confined him for six months to New Delhi in the north and for the other six to Hyderabad in the south.

He relished it when he was in Hyderabad. He could always catch the Poona Night Passenger Train and by a circuitous route negotiate the 180 miles in nine hours and arrive at the Mansion for two days a month.

This was one of those visits. He knew now that he was only touching the soil and not digging into it anymore. But he was trying to hold on to it desperately.

They sat on the artificial levee separating the lands and watched the sun rise brilliantly.

In the distance a servant plowed the land, two bullocks treading back and forth in repetitive motions. The Master, powerful, short, vigorous, handsome, with aristocratic features and a clear, radiant skin, immaculately dressed all in white muslin, wearing horn-rimmed dark glasses to avoid the rising sun, and carrying a mahogany walking stick that served many purposes, stood on the bluff. On another bluff, a slight distance away from the Master, was the little Prince in a checkered cream-colored shirt, khaki shorts, brown sandals and a safari hat. Way down below, standing, his slippers in his hand (it would be a sign of great disrespect to wear anything on his feet while taking a walk with the Master), in a slightly soiled dhoti and a torn orange shirt, in a turban brown and aged with washing in the monsoon-fed river, and a coarse wool blanket which served at times as a raincoat in the monsoon and as a bedspread when he supervised his own or the Master's farm, was Thimma, gently throwing little pieces of stone at the earth stretching in front of him.

The Master said, "Never plant a tree for yourself, ever, Thimma! No tree worth the soil will bear fruit in that short a period. It takes years—generations—for a mango tree to yield fruit. That goes for anything connected with the land."

"Then how are we going to cope with modern life, Master? Things seem to change even as you attempt to catch your balance and stand up."

"That'll be your problem, Thimma! And that'll be the problem of this young fellow, this sapling that has come out of this trunk. My grandfathers planted trees, but my father never lived to eat their fruit. He was murdered. In the same year the orchards were set on fire and destroyed. And I never have had the time to repair the damage. First I had to protect myself from being assassinated. Then I had to help protect this nation from being destroyed. In between the two tasks all I have done or been able to do is merely to hold on to the land. To the earth; to the Mansion; to the family; to Deccan. Yes, I have held on to it in spite of all provocation to go abroad; to become rich; to sell the land and capitulate. And yet without becoming bankrupt! In the last few years, all the income I have received from the land has gone to pay the taxes that the great socialist government has imposed on us. We till the land so we can keep it. Not so we can live by it. It makes us devoid of dignity."

"I've read of at least three ministers—the finance minister, the defense minister and the agriculture minister—who have not paid their taxes since India became independent."

"I know, boy, I know. But I must act unilaterally. They are ministers and I am a judge. God has given me responsibility. I must know evil so I can repudiate it. I must know evil, boy, but I must not touch it. That's the difference between us and Westerners. For them knowing is touching."

"It has been a difficult life for you, hasn't it, Master? You are not able to let go of anything; your tradition; your family name; your obligation to the country; and your commitment to a simple life."

"Yes, Thimma, my son! Even the simplest rules for a simple life must be maintained; had to be maintained. I do not smoke. I do not eat meat. The only women I have slept with have been my two wives, the one who died and the one who is now alive and has given me four beautiful sons. But look at us—you and me and Vishnoo—the Master, the son and the future prince, the three of us, sitting here like dispossessed people! How many years ago was it, Thimma, that your grandfather was the herald who escorted my father and his friends in the country to the moonlight dinner in the mango orchard beyond the stream that now separates two states? Once this land extended beyond provinces. What a fantastic event it probably was, that moonlight dinner! The food! The music! The hospitality! The tall tales! What do you see there now? Beyond the stream? Two wells, the stone parapets fallen in, broken shades and demarcations that only seem to indicate how truly barren we all have become. I don't think this place will ever turn around in the way I want it to. Not in my lifetime, anyway! And this fellow, your little Master here, he will never grow up fast enough and have children and do great things. Not in my lifetime, boy, not in my lifetime! I wonder if it does any good for good things to happen to you after you are dead?"

"You of all people, Master? You are the only person in this area who has truly believed in planting trees!"

"I don't know, son. I don't know! Look at India today. Look at what has happened to our people! Sometimes I think our sap has been drained out. We don't seem to be capable of that tremendous energy and progress that are needed to survive in a modern world. Look at the desolation around us. I gave a hundred acres away to all you untouchables! A hundred acres of good land! And now your cousin Hulaga has signed off the deed to his two acres to the loan shark across the river for ten pounds of tobacco. Two acres of land that we had for more than a thousand years are gone in less than two minutes. And now this mongrel loanshark owns my ancestral land and boasts he will get all the rest this way. I either have to go to court to get my own land back or put up with the usurper, the tobacco peddler. Do you hear me, boy?"

"Yes, Master. That's why he's a mongrel who deals with a mongrel. That's why he was born in the caste—or the castelessness —that he has been in. As the Deccan poet says, Master, 'How will the donkey ever know the value of saffron?' "

"Your learning has gone to your head, you wise fool! It's not his caste that's the problem. It's his character. He has none. And he's not the only one. Thousands of men all over the Deccan, all over India, all over our villages are like these tree stumps. Penises without a body. They live lives in desperation. Day to day. Minute to minute. They have no plans, no dreams. Only occasional fantasies. And the rich go to the movies. Oh yes! We will rise like one man or one vast zero-shaped egg to destroy a foreign government or a native dictator. But then what? In this age of individualism what will we do for ourselves? What will these people do? They blame the monsoon. They blame the earth. They blame God. They blame me. Even this fellow, this son of mine, your future Master, who fancies himself a thinker and a writer, blames me. He's fourteen years old, and he has already written a novel about village life, in which the hero marries two girls, one from the village and one from the city, and lives happily ever after on his farm. Of course, all the problems in the country have been caused by a tyrannical father who understands neither his people nor his children. It's supposed to be some kind of a socialistic novel, boy!"

Now the Master focused his eyes, directly, on the startled Prince. "What the hell do you know about life to write a novel about it, boy? Life is one hell of a complicated thing, boy! Life is tradition. Life is all this barren land. Life is all these barren people who *crumble* rather than sprout when the rain comes. Life is dealing with this archaic, visible, mirage-like reality when dreams are superimposed upon it in the form of modern machines, and transformations, and nerve-stretching, bond-breaking, death-giving, exhausting progress—birds that glide and pace and pounce upon reality like eagles and vultures, snatch the flesh and fly away with it. Yes, I recognize the energy of it all, yes, but the problem is, can we match it? Ah, dear God! Life is hoping for a second coming even when you don't believe in it and you know for certain you won't live to see it if it ever comes. Write your book, boy, but open your eyes to this vicious modern kaleidoscopic drama that whirls around us. Life is in the vast tragedies that occur in the skyscrapers of America. Life is in the desolation of the Deccan. Life is in the jungles of Africa where tyranny and democracy are equally devoid of meaning. Life is in the cold desperation of people who consume borsch. Life is all the lonely Buddhist monks who fell from the mountains of Tibet and waited to hear the world applaud their conquerors. Can you see it whole, son? Can you create the drama without any unity of time, place or action?"

The flood was overwhelming Vishnoo. He waited for the next swirl.

The Master said, "Yes, dear Thimma, my other son. My untouchable son. You are right. Yes. Yes. Yes. Vishnoo, little Prince, there is only one lasting truth. There is an organic connection among all the floating images of our world, the many islands in the stream, and you must see the connection, Vishnoo, you must. And you must appreciate it. No one before us has had to see this. Even I do not have to see it as much as you'll have to. Vishnoo, the supreme God of the Hindus! Vishnoo, my son! Can you face it? Can you accept it? Can you rebel against it? What are you going to do with it? Any fool can rebel against his father, boy. Can you shape your world? Can you shape the world of those who look up to you? That *was* my problem!"

Not too far in the distance the train from Madras wound its way towards Bombay. The smoke and the whistle and the matchbox-like red and yellow compartments disappeared into the distant trees. The young Prince sat in silence.

From his eyes tears flowed voluminously.

"I did not know I had hurt you so badly, sir! I guess all novels by sons hurt their fathers! I am sorry! I thought I was making an attempt at honest criticism. I've always felt that our greatest defect as a nation has been our inability to accept criticism from anyone. The phrase self-criticism does not exist in our languages. We might be old and we might be reverent but we are not perfect, sir!"

"Hurt, boy? Hell, no! Incensed, yes! But hurt, no! What you say now makes sense even though your book didn't. Yes. True. We are not capable of self-criticism. I probably am as guilty as you are. That's because, unlike the Westerners, we have no desire for progress. Such tangible reality is too 'materialistic' for us. You have a point, son, dear little god, Vishnoo. And maybe your *stupid* novel did too. All I ask of you is what Gautam Buddha might have asked: 'Don't look at the leg merely or the tusk alone and call the part the elephant!' Is that criticism for you, boy?"

8

man and wife

O N THE PORCH, HIS DAUGHTER was playing with white marbles. Walking up to her, he lifted her in the air, shook her, hugged her, and tickled her tiny belly so intensely with his thick crop of hair that the child began to cry. To placate her, he lighted the kerosene lamp before the usual time.

Ganga returned from the barn. He smiled at her in a spirit of reconciliation.

She dreaded the thought of sleeping with him tonight. She had always intimidated him, but secretly she was afraid of him. His intelligence. His cunning. And mad as hell about his rights over her.

"Dinner will be ready soon!" she said.

"Take your time. Do what you want from now on."

She ran into the kitchen.

He took off his tattered shirt and unrolled his turban. He rolled them together into a pillow and lay down on a jute and wood cot, a cot that was more like a hammock than a bed. He lolled in it. His daughter, little Rangi, joined him and they started swinging gently. He just wanted to lie down and let himself go.

But dinner was ready and Ganga, regaining her composure, was belligerent again. She yelled at him. Her voice was husky. The dinner was ready. Her personality was so sensual that even a rough invitation to dinner was conveyed like a sexual threat. It came floating through the darkness between him and her. He desired her. He wondered if he had ever done right by her? Was it not some essential defect in him that made her go to that *buffalo?*

Dinner was served. On a brass plate he noticed his favorite meal: hot crushed dry red pepper with a dash of peanut oil poured over it; yogurt prepared from the milk of his favorite she-buffalo, Ganga, named after his own wife; five round pieces of hot baked cornbread, called *bhakri*; eggplants fried with mustard seeds and parsley; and a raw salted onion.

Thimma dipped a piece of bread into the yogurt, put it in his mouth, and smiled at Ganga. When he grinned, Thimma looked very helpless, very much like the Master, almost like an innocent child. And if someone responded to his smile, his dark, dreamy eyes lit up with the pleasure of being recognized, and in an instant the public man became all private, all humble and ready and willing to yield.

But Ganga was accustomed to a man who either threatened her or did not say anything at all to her. She did not say much to any of her children; and much less to her husband. Even with her lover, it was more that he asked, with brute persistence, and she yielded, more out of defiance than desire. She wanted to defy her husband, with whom she could not talk, and against whom she felt a deep-seated grudge that she could not articulate. She imagined *now* that she had defied the man, Police Marya, who had wanted her. She imagined that she had mastered Marya by offering him her body at her—and not his—will and pleasure. Time had made hazy her recollection of his first violence against her. Her being accustomed to him—his body—and his growing more pliant day by day due to the inevitable attraction of her absolutely beautiful body made her feel that it had always been like this between them; that she had always twisted him around her finger.

Secretly, she knew, without a doubt, that her lover, Police Marya—big, fat, rakish and villainous as he was—wanted to fuck her and humiliate her husband. For Ganga, giving herself to Police Marya had been killing two birds with one stone. She had defied her husband and mastered his enemy at the same time.

She came onto the porch and paced up and down, waiting for Thimma to finish his dinner. Thimma did not want to be hurried. He wanted to relax. Ganga's frightening pacing intimidated him. He had meant to pay her a compliment on the delicate way she had skewered the eggplant, but now he knew that all his gallantry had evaporated into the steaming air of the Deccan warm winter night. A rare situation. Still he wanted to do some good that night. He called his daughter and within Ganga's hearing said, "Isn't your mother pretty, darling? Isn't she a pretty girl?"

He was really thinking about the first time they had walked to the river together. Years ago.

Ganga exploded like firecrackers at Deepavali. Direct compliments intimidated her as much as her pacing to and fro had intimidated him. Her breasts heaved in tension and frenzy. And he felt lust for her. She shouted: "Don't put silly and dirty ideas into the little child's head, you silly old fool! You have done enough damage already!"

He cried belligerently, "It's my child and let me play with her!"

"Are you sure it's your child? Have you ever looked at her and asked yourself why she is so dark?"

He rose from the cot. He hurled the brass plate full of his favorite meal as far as he could towards the Patel's well in the distance. The plate went flying like an ancient discus. He grabbed Ganga's dark, silky hair, unknotting the graceful bun. The flowers, the little violets, were sprinkled over the earthen floor. He tore open her blouse. He shook her wildly. He kissed her on the cheeks. Ganga, wheat-complexioned Ganga, turned red and flushed with fright. He bit her hard on the nape of her neck, he wanted to crush her Adam's apple, and with the swiftness of a cobra, he reached under her saree and sent his finger raging through her. The instant his index finger was out, he was in. Against the wall, the kerosene lamp flickering mildly in the timid wind, his little daughter watching them, he panted like the Master's horse. She tried to unstrangle herself. He felt her hot thighs, her tight, middle-aged thighs, so firm with all the hard work in the paddy fields, her big breasts bursting forth out of the torn red blouse. He came. He went. He came again. The thought that his arch-enemy had had her a few hours before excited him, maddened him to a pitch of feverishness. Ganga was no more just his wife. Ganga was some beautiful woman from a far-off land he had always dreamed of and was now touching; some exotic woman who had been mastered by someone else before; and mastering whom became absolutely essential to his personhood now. Myriad thoughts excited him once and again and then again. She could not believe his rage of passion, and yet what was not familiar was distasteful to her. Police Marya, when he came to her first, was equally distasteful to her, and now as familiarity had grown she had begun to like his huge thrusts. So this unusual man, her husband, estranged her.

At the twelfth time Ganga escaped from him and wrestled with him. She tore his hair and, crying, bit him. He fell down, a contented, vanquished man. Then he held her tightly again and pushed her forward with a swiftness that made her feel that she was going to fall off the porch. Before she knew it he had grabbed hold of her again and he was caressing her thighs with his eyes. Violently Thimma thrust his tongue into her cunt.

Ganga overflowed like the village river in the monsoon. The incredible swift activity raged in her. Hot tears of uncontrollable defeat, passion and anger scalded her cheeks. She just wanted to get hold of him!

Suddenly Thimma was totally exhausted. Like the starflies of the Deccan his stifled youth had escaped out of him to flicker only for a brief moment. Now reptile-like middle age crept up on him. He released her, pushed her away, spread his arms, and gently raising himself up to his daughter standing near the pail of water, savoring the skewered eggplant, pulled her toward him.

Little Rangi ran her fingers through his dark, slightly graying hair. Thimma kissed her. "My angel, you must truly be my mother come back to me in this reincarnation!" Then he cried, "I don't care whether she is my daughter or not! I have known her too long not to love her!"

Ganga washed her face with tepid water. It seemed to release her from her frenzy. Then she came up to Thimma. He had undressed her moments before and now it was her time to undress him. She pulled the dhoti away from him and took the bundle of his turban and his shirt, put all three together in an aluminum cooking pan and hurled it with superhuman frenzy toward the Patel's well.

Thimma was too exhausted to fight back. Rangi stared at his erect penis from close by. "Daddy, there is a boo on you." He laughed like a madman.

Ganga, shrill and angry, shouted at him.

"Get away from me, you untouchable bastard! Go back to your Master, the Brahman, who must have buggered you for thirty years. Whose prick is better? His or Police Marya's? I'll make you pay for raping me today, you bastard of the Deccan! You are not sleeping in the house tonight! I want you to get out of here right now. Take your coarse sheep's blanket and get lost. If you stay here a minute longer, I'll shout, and I'll yell, and I'll raise the whole village. You don't want your solid reputation to be hurled into the village well, do you?"

Naked, he stood listless in the dim orange light in the house. The kerosene lamplight was mild and almost extinguished. For the first time in his life he did not give a damn if anyone saw him naked. The time was near for him to become an exile from his house again.

Mildly and indifferently, he muttered, "I am going to leave, but I'm hungry. I am going to eat something before I leave."

"I am not going to bring you anything. You sent your share into the well!"

"Share, share! Everything here belongs to me, you female buffalo! It's my sweat and blood and honor. . . . Oh, forget it!"

He walked into the kitchen. There were four different cooking pans and dishes spread all around the wood stoves. The kitchen, without any chimney, was quite full of smoke. Thimma rubbed his eyes, gathered the three fat pieces of *bhakri,* poured a little peanut oil, a lot of red pepper and the skewered eggplant on them, and rolled them into a sandwich and began to eat rapidly. The hot pepper stuck in his throat and the unusually huge bite choked him. He guzzled the water, a whole tumbler of it, gulped the remaining yogurt, and murmured to himself: "I give a damn about the rest of them!" He walked back to the porch, still naked, and picked up his sheep's blanket from the huge painted wooden peg in the wall. He covered himself with it. The coarse wool scratched him. He kissed the little girl and walked out of the house.

The moon was up now. Thimma could feel the mild breeze on his face. He took quiet steps towards the river. Crickets chirped in the distance. Once again, Thimma was one with the vast, stony Deccan plateau. It stretched in front of him. Everywhere he looked, the vast moonlit sky was a lonely, huge canopy of milky whiteness.

On a clear blue-white night in the Deccan countryside, a stranger can spot anything that moves for miles. The lonely, forsaken land does not move. Very few people live in the villages, which are becoming more and more deserted. Night-strollers are always hungry for one another's company, even if the companionship lasts only a brief time. It alleviates the loneliness that creeps up on them. Out of poverty, out of frustration, out of lack of entertainment, out of boredom with familiar company, they seek out the stranger. No stranger is a stranger for long in the Deccan. It is a land full of hospitality, friendship and impossible-to-get-rid-of traditions and linguistic habits.

"Hey, hey, hey." The sound comes like a song from the distance, amid a ripple of wild laughter. "What crop do you mean to harvest, stranger, at this time of night? Whither dost thou go? On to the river, eh?" The language is formal and archaic. The conversation is played out as a repetition of past conversations among the people's ancestors. "Aren't thou afraid of ghosts hiding under the pebbles?"

"No ghosts; no voices of dead people are more frightening than the ignorant ones that walk the path of life, treading like knowing human beings," says Thimma, and adds, "You want to come and join me, young man?"

The young man, on stilts, walks with the briskness of a flying crane; a huge pole in his hand, a sheep's blanket thrown on his shoulder, just playing on the stilts with no sheep to tend to. That is the net result of desolation. He is Marya's son, Hanumantha, alias Mallik.

Thimma says, "Mallik, you look pale! Have you not been well, lately?"

"Yes, Thimma, you wise man! I've been sick and I am growing thinner by day and by night. The doctor at the railway station says I won't live but a year or so more. Can you imagine that, wiseman? I was born when you were thirty years old. And now I think I'll be gone out of here before you reap the next harvest!"

"Come, come now! Doctors are not gods. If they knew everything, why would we still be so afraid of death? I'm sure you can go to Sholapur to find a better doctor! Or even to Hyderabad?"

"The problem is, my father says, he has seven children, four by his wife, and three by his mistresses, and he does not want to spend all the money on treating one son who might die anyway. Well, I will live as long as I am going to. Maybe you can tell me a wise story on the river, old man? Can I come with you?"

"Of course you may. I've always liked you. Come with me. Let us walk in the moonlight. Let us pray for peace by the river."

9

trustee

THIMMA, LISTEN TO ME TODAY. One day I'll be gone. We Indians don't live long. I am fifty-five and I am already five years older than *the average dead Indian.* It's such a pity, though. The world is improving so fast and in some ways, so well. There must be something more than mere vulgar materialism to all the scientific progress that the Americans have made in advancing the longevity of their people. But ah! It's probably too late for people of my generation. The seeds of death have already been sown and they will sprout soon enough, much sooner than most things in life. I must accept my Indian fate.

"I want to live to be a hundred, Thimma. But I am no Soviet from Azerbaijan. I am not even that un-Indian, Police Mallanna. I am the honed-in Prince from the Deccan. The hone is the Deccan! Yes! I must set my affairs in order. There must be an equitable distribution of land. I must give up my title in my lifetime so I can see how well renunciation improves the lot of the world; the moral health of my family; my country. I trust you, Thimma. When the time comes I'll not be *buried,* like you untouchables! My ashes will disappear into the waters of the Bhima and the Krishna. They will become one not with the earth, but with the largest part of our world, water!

"And then, I want you, you *damned* untouchable, to make certain that what I have decided in life will not be contravened after my death. You and the other two lower-caste people, Hanumanth Rao of Badyal and Jimkala Mallanna—you three will be the arbiters, the true witnesses to what the Master has decided. The other two, they have integrity, probably more than you do. They are honest. But they are not as intelligent as you are. You know all the ins and outs, the castes and the communities of this area. You are the spiritual geographer of Gudur-upon-Bhima. You know what each caste and each individual is capable of. My son cannot venture

73

without you. Part of my spirit, my history, my life is in you, boy! You can recite Vedic hymns better than the family priest. You know all the stratagems that people lay in the way of honest dealing. You have laid many stratagems yourself. You have committed many little deceptions against me. But you are intelligent enough to know that when my family prospers your family will; that being a Brahman, I've appreciated in you what a Brahman should value most in himself and others—the mind, the soul. You have the Brahman mind—the mind that is capable of deception but is unwilling to perform it because it knows by intuition that the higher good is served for the individual and society when the right thing is done. When Brahmans have lost the sense of that awareness they have ruined others and themselves.

"The others of lower castes and characters do not appreciate this in you. They think of you only as cunning, which you certainly are. But you are that and something more. You know you are capable of greatness. I have only provided you with the opportunity to realize your dreams. So you want me and you will not deceive me. I've retained you and I hope my sons will have the sense to keep you. I hope they will not be so offended by your petty thieveries that they will forget the higher good!"

Thimma knew exactly what the Master was talking about. It was the regular cuts he had taken from every cart full of grain that went to the railway station bazaar. And it was not just simply that. There was a bigger deception they both knew of.

Thimma had a piece of land adjacent to the Master's on the outskirts of Kusumurthy; as a matter-of-fact, just within the borders of the ghost village, Kalla Halli, the Village Robbed. Thimma wanted the Master's land very badly but he had no intention of paying for it. He wanted the Master to reward him with it for all services he thought he had rendered. But he had never got up enough gumption to ask the Master for the reward. Rewards were given; never asked for.

When his father, Rama, died, Thimma buried him on the borderline between the two farms, his and the Master's. He told the villagers, with a slight, ironic smile, "I do not want the old man in the *center* of my farm!"

But then, at the height of the monsoon, in the dead of night, he and his sons dug up the dead man and they moved the body to the center of the *Master's* farm.

The Master, absentee-landlord that he was becoming, due to his involvement in national affairs, did not notice the new tenant of his farm until a long time after the grave had been dug there. He found out about it, accidentally, as a matter of fact, on one of his casual inspections during his summer vacations.

The Master fell back. His retinue fell behind with him. Dear God, no Brahman could ever touch an untouchable's grave! Or the plot, any piece of earth, in which an untouchable (or any person for that matter) was buried! That would be eternal pollution. Brahmans reached heaven through the other element of nature, the more dangerous one, fire.

Thimma had taken advantage of two Deccan prohibitions. First, no one was supposed to farm a piece of land on which someone was buried. Thimma knew that the Master was not about to violate that Deccan law. Second, no one could or would want to touch a land touched by an untouchable (alive or dead); let alone water it, till it, clear it.

Thimma was quite convinced that the Master would have no choice but to turn over the giant farm to him on account of it being his father's grave.

Police Marya taunted Thimma. "Don't you know you are not supposed to farm a piece of land in which someone is buried? And certainly not the one in which your own father is buried!"

Thimma said, "I've no compunctions about it. I am a modern man, Marya! I need the land. Besides, I am going to build a graveside memorial for my father. What better memorial can I build for that dedicated farmer than to make every bit of farmland productive?"

Police Marya was visibly angry at the untouchable's logic. He shouted, "What better memorial can you build for your untouchable father than to deceive the Brahman and get his land for the lowest of the low's grave? What better? Oh, you cunning bastard!"

The Master realized that Thimma had used the customs, laws and prohibitions of the Deccan to deprive him of his land. And he had succeeded.

The Master's well-known short temper was greatly aroused. He went back to the Mansion and called for Thimma immediately. This was a matter for the *Diwan-e-Khas.*

"Listen, boy!" the Master raged. "As a Brahman I'll never touch the grave of any man, let alone that of an untouchable. I will not walk on that land. You are right. But when I said I will not touch an untouchable, that includes only the dead. You! With you I have no inhibitions. You are my son, remember! As a Brahman; as a parent it is my duty to be your teacher; to chastise you for your deception."

Then, the Master thrashed Thimma with his shining mahogany stick. And grabbing hold of him, he slapped the untouchable left and right.

Thimma prostrated himself on the ground and begged the Master's forgiveness. He received the land and the forgiveness.

The Master went hurriedly to the inner bathroom with the high skylights. "I did today what Vishnoo did some time ago. I almost lost my caste. I touched the untouchable!" he told his wife.

The Master knew of several such deceptions.

But he also knew of Thimma's loyalty to the Mansion when any transaction took place between the Mansion and the outsiders.

Once it happened that a huge piece of land by the river, land that could yield hundreds of bushels of corn, became available for sale. It was considered the most fertile of all land pieces in that area. A hundred, two hundred years ago the land had belonged to the Master's ancestors. They had lost it to a loan shark for a fraction of what it was worth. Now a beautiful young widow, the granddaughter-in-law of the loan shark, had herself fallen on hard times, with the death of her young husband, and she had put up the land for sale.

Everyone wanted the piece of land. They certainly wanted to deprive the Master of it. There was a gradually spreading anti-Brahman feeling among the middle castes. They felt that the Brahmans and the untouchables were ganging up together to cut their throats. Thus it was as much pride as need of the land once owned by the Master's family that motivated the new rich.

The Master was very rueful about the land of his ancestors, but he did not have the money to make a bid. But the Master had the revenue powers of the area. He had to sign every civil transaction that occurred. Not to get involved in the matter at all, he delegated his revenue authority and his power of attorney to Sali Thimma.

The other bidders were afraid of Sali Thimma. They thought that his devious mind would find a snag, some hitch, to keep them from buying the land. All twenty of them, each one without telling the other, offered Thimma 2,000 rupees apiece. Each one of them was a descendant of the twenty who were prominent among the Sixty who had financed the Master's father's assassination. Each one of them requested a separate meeting with Thimma and each one of them invited him to his faraway well-heeled home.

"Promise me by the Saint's shrine by the river and by the truth of your father's grave," said Rudrappa, "that you will neither divulge nor acknowledge that you ever received this money."

"Promise me by the Saint's shrine by the river and by the truth of your father's grave," said Peshkar Lakshman Rao, whose father was the sole Brahman who had contributed to the Sixty, because of his dislike of the Master's father's touching the lower-caste women. "Promise me that you will neither divulge nor acknowledge that you ever received this money."

"Promise me by the Saint's shrine by the river and by the truth of your father's grave," said Khwaja Patel, the infidel, the Muslim who suspected forever that his father was perhaps the bastard son of the Master's father. "Promise me that you will neither divulge nor acknowledge that you ever received this money."

"Amazing how repetitive, unoriginal, unvarying and consistent is villainy," thought Thimma. "Only the face changes. But the innards of cowardice are always the same."

Thimma played the game. He made obsequies. He told each and every one of them, "I make promises and I keep them, great sir! No one will ever know that I ever received money from you."

No one did. When the time came, Thimma gave the 40,000 rupees he had collected to Hanumanth Rao of Badyal, the Master's house-manager, who came to the auction and bid for the Master.

The land went to the Master. It was bought with the bribe money which the bidders had conveyed to Thimma.

The Master did not know about the transaction until the Deepavali festival. Thimma interrupted the Master, who was busy lighting sparkling lights on the third floor terrace with Vishnoo and his brothers. He presented him with the deed and a bowl of rice grains on a bamboo plate, as a Deepavali gift. Then he told the Master the complete story.

"I am glad you are on my side, boy," the Master shouted and laughed in his gigantic, thunderous, unearthly, innocent way.

All such things took their time and their toll. Thimma's environment, his personality and his interests were dramatically altered. Certainly Thimma was like no other average untouchable. He still observed his manners. When the upper-caste people offered him a *beedi* or a cigarette, Thimma extended his hands as if asking for alms. The upper castes rewarded him with their support because, they reasoned, "He might be an untouchable but he knows how to keep his distance; he knows enough not to flaunt his closeness to the Master or the Brahman house."

Thimma went along with them. "Dear important people," he said. "I am an untouchable, the lowest of the low. I dare not; I would never share a meal with you higher people, upper middle-caste people. I will never dare to sit on the same train seat with you all when going to Hyderabad. Or else God will smite me."

Badyal Hanumantha Rao smiled indulgently. He appreciated Thimma even when he made fun of him. "They enjoy it, don't they," he said. "They enjoy the deference you give them. Even as they are uncomfortable with your presence everywhere, they call you 'the omnipresent man.' They refuse to believe that all such humility and abnegation and deference might be false."

"It isn't," said Thimma. "Not entirely, anyway."

Hanumantha Rao said, "They sure are proud as Deccan bulls that a super-intelligent untouchable man so close to a Brahman does not sit next to them. You have saved their caste, Thimma! You have saved them!"

They laughed together.

"Shall we see how much tadi is left still at the bamboo shop?" Hanumantha Rao asked.

"Why not? We go there so rarely anyway. Let's go."

10

traditions

THIMMA HAD BEEN LIKE NO OTHER village boy. While others measured grain, Thimma counted bank notes. Over the years the little that he knew about sowing, seeding, mowing, harvesting and barnsteading became almost nothing. When the time arrived for the Master to find out which crop to plant when, or when the winter crop was destroyed by locust or lack of rain, what spring crop to plant on top of the previous seedings, to make a profitable yield, the man to consult was no longer Thimma but the agricultural manager, Jimkala Mallanna; gentle, honest, non-controversial. Thimma's knowledge of agriculture began to be even more remote than that of the Master, who had at least not forgotten the training of his early years, the years before he went to crusade for the Mahatma.

Thimma left even his own personal farming to his oldest son, Hanumantha, who had been named so to commemorate the friendship between Thimma and the house manager of the Mansion, Hanumantha Rao of Badyal.

As time passed, Thimma became, *de facto*, the Chief of Protocol for the Master. More than anyone else, Thimma knew exactly whom the Master should meet or to whom he should grant an audience at the railway station. The first-class waiting room had to be reserved and cleaned the night before. The cobwebs had to be swept away. The ceiling fan had to be turned on early, so it would get rid of its early creaking sound and settle into an even pace by the time the Master arrived on the early morning train. Earthen jars had to be cleaned and filled with fresh water from a clean spot in the neighboring Krishna river. Clean buffalo's milk had to be found for the Master's morning tea at the railway station. The Master drank only tea prepared with hot milk and brewed with special Darjeeling leaves. Occasionally the Master would have breakfast of hot fried *puris* (puffed up to show they were fresh, and fried only in pure clean butter) and a potato *kurma* made in a sauce of lemon, parsley, turmeric, shallots, red pepper and coriander.

Once in a while a few of the Master's decrepit and bankrupt cousins from across the river, who came to see their still great cousin, would be *allowed* by Thimma to share breakfast with the Master. "We should be grateful to that untouchable sonofabitch for having a meal with our own kith and kin!" the dispossessed and irresponsible Brahmans complained behind Thimma's back to the middle-caste people.

After breakfast came the Master's audience with the local officials: the station master, the ticket inspector, the signal man, the local doctor, the sub-inspector of police, the tax collector; each and every one of whom represented, in his inimitable and cowering way, the myriad ramifications of corruption, infinite and pathetic and disgusting, and the gerrymandering powers of the gigantic Indian bureaucratic and social systems. The Master had no *de jure* power over any of them. But they all acknowledged the *de facto* social and moral influence of the Master, and they paid him homage.

For a long time, the Master, bound by tradition, customs and social inhibitions, would never eat a meal unless it was prepared by a Brahman. It was the task of Sali Thimma, the untouchable, to find a Brahman cook. Thimma did this by bribing and threatening any idiot Brahman who could make a decent meal. Only Thimma knew how to speak to the pompous, arrogant and ignorant Brahmans (who always wanted status, even when they could never back up such claim for high position with knowledge or wisdom) with a proper mixture of authority and deference—the authority was viceregal, the deference political.

Of course, as time passed, the Master relaxed his inhibitions, as did the rest of the country. Now the Master ate meals prepared by people of lesser castes who were also vegetarians, such as the traders and the phallus worshippers. It would still be a far day before the Master ate a meal prepared by a meat-eating person— a Muslim, a cane-gatherer or an untouchable.

On many of his trips, the Master was accompanied by his son, the little Prince Vishnoo, who was now in his freshman year at Osmania University. The little Prince was dying to eat a meal prepared by Thimma himself. The Prince wanted to know what kind of chef his father's most trusted man was. He even went to Thimma's house one day, unannounced, intending to demand a meal. Ever on guard against such unexpected contingencies, Thimma saw the little Prince walking in the direction of the Harijan quarters. Prostrating himself before him and importuning him to the point of embarrassment, Thimma led him back to the Brahman neighborhood.

There were other responsibilities to be handled. The protocol demanded that from each village, five people from the five major castes—the phallus worshippers, the shepherds, the cane-gatherers, the merchants and the untouchables—come to escort the Master from the railway station to the Mansion ten miles away. For ceremonial purposes they were expected to carry five axes, five ancient family swords, five clubs, five sticks and five earthen jars of water on the trip. There had to be two horses ahead and two behind the main cart. Only high officials or the Master's children could ride the horses. The Master rode in the main bullock cart, outfitted with a Kashmere rug, a Sholapur mattress and several colorful silk pillows from Gadwal and Aurangabad.

Thimma knew where to obtain an Aurangabad pillow or an 1890s ax or a Kashmere rug. If something was ever lost or stolen from the absentee landlord's house (as was beginning to happen more and more often), Thimma found a quick temporary replacement from one of the new rich shepherds or phallus worshippers in the village. Thimma knew the exact kind of pressure to put on each member of the caste who was to form the retinue for the ceremonial arrival of the Master.

Not everyone wanted to go. As the villagers became more and more independent, they preferred to eat the Master's grain while not rendering their service to him. They wanted to be independent of the Master socially, while depending on him economically. Thimma explained to them in a friendly but firm manner that the two went together.

"You cannot expect the Master to lend you money or grain without paying your respects. The Master is not a moneylender or a loan shark from the lower castes. He is a Brahman, a Prince and a Justice of the Supreme Court who spends a lot of his personal income to keep the community of villages going. This must be respected or else we will all fall apart. In these modern times we need the Master more than he needs us."

In all of Thimma's dealings, subtlety was the name of the game. Subtlety involved making the constituents recognize the threat of power with the continuous hint at the possibility that it might never be used. Even the formation of the retinue and the careful choosing of the representatives from different castes and families were not just a matter of ceremony. They involved the demonstration, visible and unequivocal, of the Master's power. It was to make clear that all the members of the retinue were open supporters and followers of the Master. The Master's support came from his people, and from the exercise of protocol over the petty bureaucrats at the railway-station town. It was a clear indication that the Master was the master of all the area around him. All the sources of power, official or unofficial, were linked to him, the super powerhouse. His was the privilege of being heard but not seen.

It would be wrong to assume that the villagers paid respect to the Master because he was such a well-known man in faraway Hyderabad or New Delhi. The villagers had a saying: "We respect a man who is the inspector of police at Krishna-upon-Bhima more than the Indian envoy to Turkey."

For the villagers, reality was here; in the convoluted, scorched, barren, tear-filled, funny, ancestral Deccan. No matter what anyone did in any other corner of the world, the man had to prove himself once again on his native ground; he had to prove that he could keep power before he could have it. They respected the Master (even when, occasionally, they grew chary of the ceremonies) not because he was a Supreme Court Justice, but because he knew how to override all the internecine caste permutations and combinations and to arrive at equitable solutions without tipping the social balance. The Master and his ancestors had ruled for two thousand years and more by indirection, on a set of principles that combined compassion, fair play and a sense of being answerable to God for the rightness of one's actions.

That was why the villagers had respected and feared the Master. That was why they respected and feared his agent, Sali Thimma. Thimma was the perfect viceroy. The untouchable understood the spirit and the letter of the Master's power.

That, in fact, was why the little Prince had rebelled against his father in the first place. That was why he had written his socialistic novel. The little Prince wanted to sweep away all the old systems, the castes, the classes, the connecting links; sweep them away without Marxism. The little Prince wanted to start a new world where everyone would be everyone's equal and Indians

would feel a sense of community with themselves and with all of
mankind in a modern, intellectual, intelligent Utopia.

"If you can do it I will not prevent you, boy," said the Master.
"Realism is not the only key to the world, although it has opened
more doors, all through history, than any other."

In reality, the Master did not hold any particular official
position in the villages. The village administration consisted of five
people, the *panchayat*. There was the revenue collector (the title
held by the Master's ancestors, in addition to their rank of prince).
There was the trader. There was the sheriff or the police patel (the
position Marya and his father, Police Mallanna, and his father and
father's father, had always held). The police patel collected a police
tax (also called, occasionally, a criminal's tax), filed charge sheets
against accused persons, prepared reports on crimes committed,
accepted complaints, settled disputes, and escorted to the district
or state police station people who were under arrest—people who
threatened others or who committed any illegal or immoral act such
as theft of a godown, burning-down of a barn, or abduction of a girl.
And then there was the village untouchable, who sat on the council
but did not sit with them. The untouchable's job was to arrange for
the beating of drums—wild, barbaric and almost apocalyptic—at
all festivals and funerals of the lower classes (the Brahmans took
their dead to the cremation ground in solemn, unearthly silence),
the cleaning of garbage and cowdung in the villages, the butchering
of pigs for the lower castes, and the flaying of dead animals for
footwear. Last but not least there was the representative elected by
all the people, a sort of delegate-at-large, who was usually the most
popular, irreproachable, non-controversial, the most sober of all
the villagers: in this case it was the Master's agricultural manager,
Jimkala Mallanna.

Had the Master retained his ancestral position of revenue
collector, he would have had to go to all the meetings of the
panchayats of several villages and sit with the others as equals. For
two hundred years or more now, none of the Master's family had
ever done that, except when they were financially very low. This
had happened a few times in the past, owing sometimes to the
family's own mismanagement. At other times, unscrupulous neighbors took advantage of adolescent heirs shouldering family responsibility prematurely, owing to deaths, assassinations, poisonings or
the delinquencies of their parents. So every time a man from the

Master's family sat on the councils, it indicated that the Master's family was not in such good financial shape, and accordingly the family's power in the councils diminished.

Being out of the council the Master had more power than if he were of it. Now all the five members were beholden to him. The Master still held the revenue collector's office in name, but he delegated his power of attorney to Hanumanth Rao of Badyal, who took all the income (the monthly honorarium paid by the government and the official commission made on every civil transaction) and deposited ten percent of it in the Master's account.

In village politics the Master was what the Mahatma was in national politics. On paper Gandhi held no position at all. Gandhi was not the President of India. Gandhi was not the Prime Minister of India. Gandhi was not the Home Minister of India. But all three trekked to Gandhi's *hut* regularly, before they made any decisions of any importance. No one took his seat in Gandhi's hut before touching the feet of the great man. It should be emphasized, of course, that Gandhi did not demand that any of this be done. It was purely voluntary. It was the way in which a patriarchal society functioned. The country needed Gandhi. The villagers needed the Master.

Part Three

11

little prince

O NE DAY, THE LITTLE PRINCE, author of the unfortunate novel
about the socialistic transformation of India and the abortive
theory of international brotherhood, decided to pay a surprise visit to his father, who was vacationing at the Mansion.

It was the middle of summer and the height of the mango
season.

The Prince took the passenger train from Hyderabad at eight
P.M., and slowly counting all the tiny moffusil stations that passed
by, he dissipated. In the middle of the night he got off at Wadi
Junction, had a cup of pale brown tea and some stale *samosas*, and
stared at the piles and piles of Shahabad marble hoarded on the
other side of the railway tracks. At one-thirty in the morning the
passenger train arrived from Poona, bound for Raichur, and the
Prince got into the third-class compartment. As a young scholar at
Osmania University, the Prince was not in a position to travel first
class.

Still in his pajamas, the prince dozed off. It is a very lonely
stretch, the two-and-a-half-hour trek from Wadi Junction to the
Krishna railway station. At four-thirty in the morning, while it was
still dark, with the guard drinking tea and eating his biscuits at the
teastand by the tree, the coolies running to load baggage, and the
local postman coming to collect the mail from Poona, one of his
neighbors in the train awakened the Prince in a frenzied hurry and
literally pushed him onto the platform as he hurled his baggage
after him. The train left the platform and rolled off beyond the iron
bridge across the Krishna river—the bridge that the Prince's
grandfather, as an enterprising young engineer-contractor, had
built in 1893. The Prince attempted to wake up. In his Hawaiian
slippers, striped pajamas, unkempt hair and thick beard, the Prince
looked more like a country bumpkin, who had just learned to
discard his traditional Indian dress, than like a Prince.

The Prince, in common with all male members of his family, had an eleven o'clock shadow. The rumor in the countryside was that all the hairy princes were vigorous babymakers. Their thick and ever-growing hair was considered an indication of their seminal vitality.

Soon the stalls closed. The next train would not arrive until noon. There was no one left on the platform. The station master at Krishna-upon-Bhima was also doubling as ticket inspector. He came up to the little Prince and demanded his ticket.

The Prince searched for his ticket. It was gone. Everything was gone: his ticket, his wallet, his money in the side pockets. The Prince was mortified.

The stationmaster was new at his job. He had been transferred from the North. He knew nothing of the Deccan and its customs and its rulers. He assumed that every man arriving at the station, which he had named the Sahara, was either a country bumpkin or a friend of one, out to trick him and take advantage of his being new. Certainly out to deceive the Indian Railways!

"You think I'm going to fall for the oldest trick in the book, you oily bastard?" he screamed, and kicked the Prince.

The Prince, shocked, was totally immobilized.

"All you country bumpkins are alike!" he shouted. "You travel on trains without tickets and then you attempt to deceive me and the Indian government and act innocent. Sure you lost the ticket! Sure, sure! How did you manage to board the train at Wadi Junction? That's what I don't understand! You must have caught the speeding train near the Public Gardens as it was nearing the Husain Sagar lake. I'll teach you the lesson of your life, you son-of-a-bitch! You think you can cheat me? Sure you are the son of a Prince, and I am the King of Kashmere! What the hell are you talking about being a Prince? There are no princes in India any more and there certainly never were any in the Deccan. I know more about Deccan than you do, bastard!"

The Prince wanted to remind him that the most magnificent and the most impregnable fort in the world, the Golconda, was built by a Deccan prince for the Deccaners. And by Deccan ingenuity! But he was too humiliated to speak.

The stationmaster locked the single wrought-iron gate that let passengers out to the railway town. Then, pushing and shoving the little Prince, he escorted him into the huge, elaborate waiting room that had eighteen-foot ceilings built by the British long ago for the Nizam of Hyderabad. It was the same formal room in which the Prince's father always conducted his business at the railway station and gave audiences to people, including, in the past, dozens of stationmasters.

The stationmaster pushed the Prince into the bathroom, that was deodorized by mothballs and dimly lighted by petromax lamps. He made the Prince sit on a stone seat meant for bathing. Then he locked the bathroom with a huge Godrej lock and walked away. He had been so very incensed simply because he felt he could not take such *lying* in the early hours of the morning, of all times! He had to deal with it all day and all week: the importunings of the miserable villagers; the countless ticketless travelers. Besides, his wife of two years had left him yesterday and gone back to the city because she could not stand the loneliness of the railway station and the desolation of her husband's work.

The Prince sat on the hole in the floor built of exquisite Shahabad marble for British officials of the Victorian and the Georgian eras. And he cried profusely. His egalitarian soul blinked; and remained petrified as a Gudur cat. The Prince wished that someone would know that he was the son of the Master and not a petty common thief or a village bumpkin. He wondered, while shitting involuntarily, what would happen to a common villager who was not educated, if he really and truly did lose his ticket. He was finding out. He was so scared of being humiliated by the station master that he became afraid of flushing the toilet loudly. He sat there in misery.

He noticed the huge Victorian French window of the bathroom. Stealthily he unlatched it. Outside, the morning sun seemed to be rising from the faraway Bay of Bengal. In front of him were several bullock carts tied to little posts, and sitting in front of the carts was Police Marya, with a huge shining silver necklace around his neck, a shiny white dhoti, a white Nehru shirt, and a sparkling red silk turban that they called the *rumal* in the Deccan. Surrounding Marya were villagers: his workers, servants, sharecroppers and hangers-on—in short, his retinue. Chewing on tobacco, Marya was regaling his followers with a wild tale. From the giggling, embarrassed look on their faces, the Prince guessed that the tale had something to do with Police Marya's many, quite real, sexual exploits.

Holding on to the shutters of the window tenuously, the Prince craned his neck outside and cried: "Marya, Marya, Marya!"

Marya turned around as if he had heard the voice of God himself. He looked around, and there was the young Prince's neck hanging down like that of a pathetic sow in Thimma's pig stockade.

"Let the bull be fucked a hundred times," Marya shouted and ran up to the French window in complete amazement. When he reached there, Marya laughed hoarsely, wildly, hilariously.

"That's very funny, little Master! That's very funny! What are you trying to do? Is this something new they teach you in college?"

The Prince explained in detail what had happened to him.

Marya was utterly incensed. His face became livid with uncontrollable rage.

"That cow-sucking, mother-fucking, my-ass-licking northern bastard!" he shouted. "Master, please get down and shut the window, sit in the bathroom and be quiet! I'll get you out in a minute."

And then Police Marya gathered his gang: his untouchables with their axes; his shepherds; his merchantmen; and his six cousins.

They walked into the third-class waiting hall. The others stared wistfully at the colorful posters: "Visit Kashmere," said one poster, and showed a pretty Kashmere girl in tight clothing and a half-open veil navigating a little boat full of fruit and flowers. Marya's cousin looked at the poster and massaged his penis. There were other posters: "Visit Hyderabad, the Home of Golconda"; "Visit Khajuraho, the Erotic Paradise"; "Visit Bombay"; "Visit Madras"; "Visit Delhi, the Capital of India"; "Visit Varanasi, the Holy City." The villagers waited, while smoking their *beedis* prepared from tobacco stolen from the Master's godown.

Marya went to the ticket counter. The stationmaster was sending some signal in Morse code to a neighboring station.

"Give me a ticket!" shouted Marya.

"Where to?"

"To heaven, you fool, where else?"

"Get lost, you village idiot! Or I'll call the police."

"*You'll* call the police, you third-rate northern bastard who drinks the piss of the pig? *You're* going to call the police? I *am* the police! I am Police Patel Marya and my forefathers have been the police in this area for three hundred years. You want to call the sub-inspector of police? You! Open the damn gate and let us in, in a minute, or we will break this window down and get your hide." Marya's entourage rushed up to the ticket window. Within a second the stationmaster knew they were going to do it.

He shut the Morse code off. "Please, please, I am looking for the keys," he muttered, and in a flash ran out of his office, turned the corner onto the platform, and the huge gate separating the platform from the town was flung open like the gate to a temple in the early morning.

They walked up to him. Marya twisted the stationmaster's ear. The huge, six-foot-two man, in humiliation, grimaced uncomfortably. Marya twisted his moustache. Marya tickled him.

"Please! The next train is to arrive soon. If I don't send the signals on time there might be a huge wreck at the station. What do you want from me?"

"Open that damn door! Let's go in there."

"That's a first-class waiting room. That's for railway officials. Gazetted officers. Ministers. Police people. Or high people."

"What the hell do you think I am, a low person? You creepy bastard from nowhere! Where the hell do you come from? And then *you* want to insult us! Open the damn door!"

The stationmaster opened the door. The old Victorian ceiling fan was still whirring.

A bug jumped from one end of the timber couch to the other.

"Why is this damn bathroom door locked?"

"Hey, who are you anyway?"

"I'll show you who we are. I'll teach you a lesson you'll never forget. You think every person around here is a crook and you are so high and mighty, don't you? Damn, open the bathroom door!"

"What do you intend to do?"

"What do I intend to do!" And Marya raged hoarsely, showing his thirty-two shiny teeth. His black eyes turned red. "I am going to take you in there, take off your stupid official white pants, take some warm Deccan peanut oil, rub it on you, and fuck your goddamned ass. And when I'm finished so will everyone else: including those damned untouchables there; including this bastard, this cousin of mine who was massaging his penis looking at some damned railway poster." And then Marya spit at the stationmaster.

The stationmaster was as immobilized and petrified on entering the bathroom as the Prince had been before. The Prince looked up, glad to see the outside world, and rushed out to the waiting room, lest he might be locked in again.

"Don't sit on that couch, little Master, let me clean it up for you." And Police Marya unwound his shiny red silk turban and wiped the dusty couch with it. In a flash he killed the bug and threw it away onto the railroad tracks. Then he begged the Prince to sit down. A boy rushed up to get some fresh drinking water from the Krishna river. Another fellow offered to press the Prince's legs.

The egalitarian Prince refused. He asked Marya to sit next to him on the couch.

"I don't even smoke in front of the great Master, little Prince," Marya said, slightly uncomfortable at the Prince's desire for intimacy; equality. Then he held the stationmaster with his huge hands.

"Would you like to kick him, Master?"

"Heavens, no!"

"Then let me do it, little Prince. You have delegated the authority."

First Marya slapped the stationmaster hard on the face and then he kicked him in the buttocks. The confused man, the green flag still in his hand, rolled over like a football. He stood up again, gained his equilibrium and said, "Are you finished?" and proceeded to sit on the chair.

"Ah! Ah! You don't sit there. Nobody sits in any chair as long as the Master is around. Is that clear?"

The sub-inspector of police was called.

He came and saluted the Prince. Then he gave orders.

"Yes! Constable Ibrahim! Be sure to get the best tea made out of pure milk for the little Master here!"

Marya explained to the stationmaster. "The Doctor, the Postmaster and you—the Stationmaster—are all behind the Sub-Inspector of Police in rank. You salute the S.I. and you obey him. And he and anyone above him obeys the Master. While the Master is not there you obey the little Master, and when the little Master is not there you obey me!"

In spite of himself the Prince was fascinated by Marya's powers of usurpation; his mastery of raw power. Marya usurped viceregal functions, though there never had been any such delegation from the Master. The matter had never been resolved.

Marya arranged for the best available bullocks full of decorations and bells to be tied to the best available cart and then he escorted the Prince and the cart towards Gudur-upon-Bhima.

12
turnabout

THE PRINCE HAD BEEN CONFOUNDED, relieved, pleased and appalled by Police Marya's exercise of power. He wondered what kind of manager Marya would make? He must certainly inform father of how Marya had restored his dignity, arranged for his breakfast, and paid for the rental of the bamboo cart.

"How is your father, old man Mallanna, doing these days?"

"He's dead, little Master. He died three weeks ago at the age of one hundred and three, leaving me with a thirteen-year-old half-brother! Can you believe that old goat's gumption? Now he has left a thirty-six-year-old horny, healthy, vigorous wife whom no one can take care of. For who can compete with a hundred-and-three-year-old dead man? Everyone would feel that he was sleeping with his grandfather's wife, if you know what I mean?"

"He didn't like our family very much, did he?"

"No, Master, he didn't. He resented you for being a Brahman. He resented you for having all the power. He resented the old Master for giving up his position as record-keeper of the villages. He resented the old Master for not sitting as an equal with him in the *panchayat.* He resented the old Master because the people in the villages loved him. He used to say angrily: 'I have all the sex. And the old Bomman has all the love.' "

"Do you resent us too, Maranna?"

The young Prince was using a term of affection and respect. In Kannada, Anna means older brother. Marya blushed in deep gratitude.

"I don't know, Master. I really don't know. I don't think I hate you or your father or the old house. No, I don't. My father always told me to hate, but I could never bring myself to do it. Those tales of hatred and revenge seemed to be so much from the past, from the times of Rama and Krishna. But I do resent one thing, dear Master! I cannot understand why the old Master, a great man, born in such a noble family, and in such a first-rate caste, takes to his heart the lowest of the low, the man *I* wouldn't touch—the untouchable. That burns me up, sir, that burns me to hell. I think that's a great injustice done to all of us upper-caste people, a great slap in the face, telling us I don't give a damn about you and your caste and your position in society. What an insult! My God! They say a curse is upon these untouchables. They committed great misdeeds in the past; in their previous lives; so now God has separated them from us. They cannot even drink the water from the same well as we do, Master. They say if a Brahman violates the rule of God and the system that HE has established, grief will come to the family."

"You don't believe that, do you?"

"Of course I do, Master. That's God's will."

"Come on now, Marya! Don't you think Thimma is equal to all of us and in many ways even superior to us?"

"Of course not! You should know better than that, little Master! That untouchable's brain in his head is a curious abnormal thing! It's a human being come out of a buffalo!"

"I like Thimma, Marya! I like him very much. But I like you too, especially after what you did for me, even though not in the way you did it. I'll try not to think of the fact that your father arranged for the murder of my grandfather. I want to ask father if he can appoint you one of his managers."

"Yes, Master, I'd like that. As long as my father was alive I could hardly come near the house. But now I want to."

The retinue crossed the five streams, the difficult curves, the brown earth which indicated the land was in the state of Andhra Pradesh, and came to the dark earth which indicated that they had entered the state of Karnataka and were not too far from the Mansion. They arrived at the Mansion before dinnertime.

The Prince went directly into a conference with his father in the open-air receiving hall on the third floor. He explained his rescue and his plans to hire Police Marya.

The old Master exploded like a thousand tons of vintage Golconda gunpowder.

"That bastard, that thief, that criminal! You want to hire him? You know how long it has been since he repaid a penny of all the money, a grain of all the corn, a piece of all the goods that we have lent him to develop his goodwill? An eternity! He hasn't paid a penny back of anything he has borrowed. He lied about his desperations; his son's health; his wife's miscarriage. He never returned anything voluntarily on any due date. When we sent our servant to collect, in a civilized, understated way, what did Marya do? He beat him up! He set fire to our assistant manager's barn, so now the poor fellow does not dare go near him. When Hanumanth Rao of Badyal went to collect our credits, this bastard, this Police Marya, with the help of his peasant friends, in the middle of the night, gathered all his grain, loaded it in carts, and whisked it away to the railway station. Then he claimed he had no food to eat and certainly no grain at all to repay his loans. They would have to wait until harvest time, next year! He told one of our bookkeepers that *I* had given him permission to borrow two of our bullocks for his plowing. And he sold them off at the spring fair at Gudeballur. And now he says he will repay even that 'loan' in good time!

"All this could be forgiven if he had the decency to repay his debts in services. In Deccan barter is of many kinds. But he hasn't spent a single day or a single night supervising our farms at sowing, plowing, seeding or harvesting time. He hasn't organized a single caravan of carts to haul our goods to the railway station. He hasn't made a single decision or committed a single deed that has brought me profit or comfort. When he was sixteen I thought there was some hope for him as there was for the other three. But I tell you, son, a dog's tail is always twisted. It's his heredity. Look at his father and the *great* deeds he committed! Most important of all, most important of all, God damn it, where the hell is that bastard?"

From the top of the third floor, the Master shouted down at Police Marya who, as usual, was sitting on the platform by the artesian well and regaling his listeners with tales of masculinity.

"Hey, you bastard Police Marya, come into the house! Come into the receiving hall, damn it; you others, hold him and bring him down here!"

The voice was like a hundred thunders from the Deccan sky.

Marya, petrified, ran into the Mansion. The Master came down to the receiving hall. His famous mahogany stick went wild in his hands. His temper was uncontrollable.

He walked up to Marya. And he blasted him with the stick on every part of his body, as he lambasted him with words.

"You bastard! You want to serve in my house? You are not fit to eat the refuse in the outhouse! You low, cunning rodent!"

And then he kicked Marya in the buttocks.

Marya lost his balance and fell onto the marble floor. The Master got on top of him like a little child, and pounding him with his feet, he jumped all over Marya's body. Then he ordered Marya to stand up.

The old Master was only five feet three and about one hundred twenty pounds. Police Marya was over six feet tall and about three hundred pounds. But Marya stood trembling in the receiving hall. The Master pulled Marya's dhoti away.

Naked, his massive penis surrounded by lush, black pubic hair, trembling, shaking but almost proud, unable to comprehend the twist of destiny today, Marya wondered what would happen next.

"I'll have your phallus cut off, you do that again, you low Deccan animal! Get the hell out of here! Walk from here to Kusumurthy naked! Get out of my sight! You know why I am so angry! You know what you have done!"

Three men knew what Police Marya had done but none acknowledged it openly.

It had happened on the day that the Master was outlining his plans for the division of the property. He had told Thimma, "When my ashes are in the Bhima River, remember that you will be one of the executors, arbiters of my estate. I have eight children, four from the first wife, who is dead and gone, almost thirty years now, and four from the second. In olden times daughters never received any property. I don't believe in that. But my daughters and their husbands are not going to get any property from here either. The reason is simple and clear: I have given to them enough in jewelry, in money and in other ways as dowry and as gifts. That balances out the potential value of these lands. It's nothing more than symbolic at this period in my life.

"I went to great pains to do this—to be fair and equal. I broke my back to give enough in kind to my daughters; for the land cannot, should not, go to anyone who does not carry the Gudur name. That's the way it has been for three thousand years. That's the reason for these efforts and these decisions. Not sex but name. It's your duty to protect the interests of my sons at all costs." And laughing greatly he added, "Or I'll destroy you from heaven!"

Thimma had been pondering the fatefulness of all the decisions that night. The Master's wife, whom Thimma called "mother," served him with her own hands (it was the highest honor an untouchable could receive from a Brahman), and all vegetarian food too, delicately prepared in a subtle balance of vegetables, corn and spices. This was quite unlike what happened to others when they visited the Mansion on duty. The others were assigned to dine at the houses of various peasants in the village of Gudur and the tab was picked up by the Master.

At eleven o'clock Thimma decided to walk back to Kusumurthy five miles away. On the way he crossed a village, two great and ancient temples, two streams, and two banyan trees that served as distance-markers.

To himself, Thimma sang an old song which was partly funny and partly melancholic, about the mating of the beauty and the beast, a song written by the famous Kannada erotic poet of the ninth century, Janna. The lines went:

Verily like a crow which, having tasted the neem,
Finds the mango tasteless, did the queen,
Her affections engaged to the ugly one,
Find her interest in the king on the wane.

Like a bee caught in a blue nocturnal lotus,
Happy to find release at the fall of dusk,
From the arms of the king mimicking sleep,
Softly the queen stole to the trysting place.

Lo! Like a hawk swooping upon a hapless swan,
By her braid the uncouth one caught the queen,
And the scents, perfumes and betel in the platter,
As he knocked her down, scattered helter-skelter.

Like a farmer beating fiber did the bastard
Kick the innocent queen holding her braid;
Though bruised and bleeding like a viper caned,
She squirmed at his feet and began to plead.

O! My love! It is true I tarried, but without cause
Would I? That loathsome interloper did hold me, alas,
In amorous sport most unwelcome and overstay I did
Albeit without heart! Without a blush was she candid.

.   .   .

Homicidal thoughts banished, the king returned,
And feigning sleep lay in his uneasy bed;
The queen followed and lay by his side,
Thinking it was the sleep of the tired.

The lovely queen who had embraced the wretch
To the king was now a thorn in the flesh;
As a pot of milk is spoiled by a drop of lemon
Or honey in the company of water, so was the queen.

Pity the irony of fate! That so lovely a queen,
Wedded to so handsome a king, should seek so hideous a mien!
Were I to meet fate face to face, I would cut off its nose
And let it wander pitilessly with bloody woes!

And so to Maridatta telling the tale
Abhayaruchi summed up its moral:
When fate unites with Cupid's tricks,
Man invites mockery's pricks.

The dark, rocky river Bhima rumbled in the distance. The monsoon clouds gathered above. It rained. It poured. Thimma ran to the temple on the farm and took shelter.

During the same period, Police Marya was roaming the village.
He decided to walk into the untouchables' quarters when Thimma was not there.
He walked up to Thimma's house.
Ganga, the absolutely beautiful, fair, wheat-complexioned,

lotus-eyed, big-breasted, slim, reed-waisted wife of Thimma was sitting on the porch and sorting out stone particles from the rice. Marya walked up to her and just stared at her daringly.

Startled, Ganga stood up. Half-covering her eyes with her scant saree, she muttered: "He's not here. No one is here. The older sons are farming. The young one is at the temple listening to the epic of Rama."

"That's why I came," Marya said. "For the next two hours no one is going to be around."

He walked close to her, he bent down, and forcibly he held her hand. Her bangles jangled and Ganga turned tense. Marya flipped his dhoti aside and shoved her hand onto his penis. It was huge, and it was alien. Ganga stared at him in terrified fascination! She had heard about him. He was reputed to have had every girl in the village that he had ever wanted.

But he had never come to the untouchables' quarters.

Not until today.

There was thunder outside and the rain fell heavily.

"It's the monsoon," Marya said and pushed her into the single inner room. There were sacks of corn piled up against the walls. From the skylight very little light shone. Marya pushed her against the sacks, and soot and dust spread in the room. Then he grabbed for every part of Ganga's body, her buttocks, her back, her long dark hair, her thighs. He parted them and fucked her with blasting energy. And then in anger and frustration, he cried, "Thimma thinks he has power, but I've what's in between these thighs! Yes I do! You are going to want me from now on. Day after day after day."

Even as he said so and thrust inside her, Ganga arrived at the realization that yes, she was going to want him, his dark, huge body, and his fascinatingly fierce, shiny face. She crushed him between her thighs.

When the rain stopped Marya was gone.

Thimma returned to the house. As usual he talked about the Master and the farm and the land and the children and what he was going to do about his dreams. He told her that he felt sad when the Master talked of dying. There could never be another man like the Master, not for the untouchables, anyway. Never again.

Ganga cried.

Thimma took off his turban and lay down on the jute cot. Ganga lay down next to him and held onto his penis. Thimma had fallen asleep. She caressed him and she sucked him. She remembered the first time she had sucked him among the river rocks.

He came, but he did not know he had.

She cried.

"You are finished, you bastard, you are!"

The next day, Police Marya found an untouchable boy playing by the river. Marya offered the boy a quarter and asked him to deliver a piece of paper to his aunt. "If you open the paper or let anyone else other than your aunt touch it, I'll cut your *lingam* off, you understand!" The frightened boy was very careful.

Ganga read the note: "Meet me by your father-in-law's grave as soon as your husband leaves for the Mansion. Signed—the man who fucked you last night and the man who will fuck you this afternoon!"

At nine o'clock in the morning, Thimma ate his meal of hot cornbread, butter, red pepper and cucumber curry, and left for the Mansion again. By eleven o'clock, the two older children left to work for the farmer who had hired them, and the little boy went to play by the river.

Ganga fixed a picnic of cornbread, onions, garlic and fresh buttermilk, and went to her father-in-law's grave.

The corn in the field was higher than a man.

The Village Robbed was without a single person in sight.

Police Marya flung her down on the muddy earth and he pushed himself into her mouth.

Later they ate the picnic she had brought.

That night Thimma was later than usual coming home.

"It rained heavily again tonight," he said, walking in. "The Master had something more to discuss. He's leaving for Hyderabad tomorrow."

He got into their bed.

"Don't sleep next to me!" Ganga shouted.

"What's the matter? Are you angry with me again?"

"No! But you are dirty. Your feet are full of the monsoon mud. I don't think you are going to take a bath tonight. And I don't want to sleep next to a dirty man!"

"That sounds fair," said Thimma and rolled off to sleep.

He dreamed of his wife and he came.

Next morning Thimma went to see the Master off at the railway station. On his return, he said, "I'll have to go to Hyderabad next week. The Master needs my advice. He needs me. I think if I can untangle the partition problem, I'll have risen and escaped my curse as an untouchable."

"You'll always be an untouchable! Even to me!"

Thimma's mind was far away.

"You know, Ganga, I've been thinking of giving up sex altogether. They say it conserves your energy and your life. I was reading in the Mahatma's autobiography, the other day, and he supposedly gave up sex altogether with his wife, when he was only thirty. Maybe I can do that!"

"What are you going to do with *it*? Give it to the nation? Or the Master?"

Thimma frowned at her.

Part Four

13

ganga

O NE DAY GANGA BEGAN WALKING to her father-in-law's grave
again.
One of her husband's cousins accosted her. "What are
you doing in the farm every day, sister? Your husband is away and
your children are working on other people's farms."

"I'm fucking with Police Marya. One day when my husband
was gone, Marya came to our house, and he forced me, and he
fucked me in the store room. Then he asked me to meet him here
every afternoon. That's what I'm doing."

The other woman pressed her fingers into her ears. "Chhee,
chhee, chhee! Oh, sister! What has come over you? How can you
talk like that? You speak like a slut. What are you talking about?
Are you angry with your husband? I've never seen you talk like
this before!"

"I've never been in a situation like this before. I speak like
a slut because I am one. You can become one too if you want to.
He fucks real good!"

"My God! I've my husband. I don't need no damned middle-
caste man. I told your husband not to get mixed up with all those
big Brahmans and their big matters. It's not for us. When an
untouchable uses his brains too much he's sure to lose his mind
and his house. Anyway, I don't believe a word you say, sister! I
think you are trying awfully hard to take revenge on somebody. No
one can do such a thing and talk about it!"

"You can come and watch if you want to!"

"Heaven forbid!"

Ganga walked towards the farm. And her cousin followed her.
She watched. Astounded and repulsed, and burning with anger, she
came back and she told her husband.

Her husband exploded. "Even if that bastard Thimma cannot
protect his own bed, we cannot let this happen to our caste and our

community! These upper-caste assholes have fucked us enough in
the past! I am fed up with the damned Brahmans! I am fed up with
the damned middle-castes! I am going to kill that bastard Police
Marya if he sets foot in our quarters! I am going to, I tell you!"
But Marya never did.

Ganga did not go to the upper-caste area either.

They met always near the grave in the Village Robbed, where
Thimma had seen his father's ghost crying for revenge.

Thimma's cousins (who were all the untouchables in the village) congregated and conferred.

They felt extremely upset, castrated.

They collected their axes, their rusty antique nineteenth-cen-
tury swords, their pikes and shovels, their clubs and sticks, and
decided to attack Police Marya's house.

Marya was ready. He had heard the news. He wanted such an
opportunity to prove once and for all that he was indeed superior
to Thimma; to the untouchables. He gathered his cousins and
brothers, even those from the neighboring villages. He shouted, "I
want a battle-royal, damn it! I want to vanquish the untouchables
in an open contest and prove to Ganga, my favorite untouchable
cunt, how much of a man I am both in and out of her. I have enough
money to bribe the Sub-Inspector of Police. And to buy the rifles."

Thimma came back to the village. He noticed the axes his
young nephews were carrying around. He noticed the hidden
swords and the concealed clubs. He called the five oldest men to
the banyan tree. And there he yelled: "What do you think you are
doing? You want all our children to be killed?"

"Oh, oh, you cockless bastard! What do you know about the
pride of the children, you no-good worthless authentic one-hun-
dred-percent Brahman shit! You ask us what we are doing, you
goddamned untouchable sonofabitch? You perpetuate the slavery
of the ages with your perverted learning and you ask us what we
are doing? We ask you why you haven't done a damn thing so far?
In the name of Maramma, the untouchables' goddess, we ask you
why? Do you know who is fucking your wife? Do you know what
a nose-cutting job has been done on us? Have we not been low
enough in life already? When are you going to stand up as a man?"

"Never! I am not a man anymore if being a man means
sacrificing your children for your pride! I know what your manhood
has done to you all! It has destroyed countless children who could

have grown up to be something! You think I don't know what has happened? You think I am blind? I have seen it. I have known it. But I am not Police Marya. I have no need to prove myself to everyone. Yes! I've turned the other cheek. If it made Ganga happy to do what she did let her do it. I thought about it; I decided what was more important; and I knew that by preserving the Mansion, I would bring happiness to more numbers of people than by simply incensing you all to revenge! You get into a fight with them and they will pulverize you. And not one of you, *men* or children, will be left to tell the story. The police will not even accept a complaint. They did not even punish the people who murdered the great Master's father! They knew full well who they were! The best thing is to do something positive. That's what the philosophy of this nation teaches us! That's what the great men and women of our culture have told us!"

"Screw your culture and screw your great men! Fuck the culture which tells us always to be humble and low! To hell with your philosophers! To hell with your nation, you idiot! To hell with Gandhi and Nehru and Buddha and the Master! Does it not hurt you, you goddamned untouchable bastard cousin of ours? You who have a dead thorn for a cock?"

"You ask me if I don't hurt when I am betrayed? You ask me if I don't bleed when I am cut? Oh! Oh! Oh! Like the cobra's bite it stings me! Like the hound's tooth it gnaws me! Like the Deccan bull's horn it pierces me! Yes! Yes! Yes! But these tears are nothing! Yes! I am going to rise above it, I tell you I am. It's a matter between me and my wife!"

"No, it's not! If you are going to live in this community you will live with honor. Do you know she's carrying *his* child?"

"Yes, I know. What else are you going to tell me?"

The group got together. It decided.

"Ganga will take a long vacation from the village. She will go across the river to her Kristen parents. She fits well with them anyway! They tell us that the people in the West, all the Kristens, indulge in daily adultery, irresponsible sex and violent sexual orgies. That's just like them damned Kristens!

"And Thimma! You and your children are banished from the untouchable quarters. You are not fit to be an untouchable!"

14

separation

THIMMA AND HIS CHILDREN LEFT the village.

They moved to a farm in the area of Kalla Halli, the Village Robbed, and there they built a hut by the curve of the river.

This was the place where he had first fallen in love with Ganga. This was the ghost village on whose borders his father was buried. This was the village on whose borders, desolate, Ganga had betrayed him day after day. This was the village where his father's ghost had cried for revenge. This was the village where no one lived except Thimma and his family, the banished untouchables.

Thimma dreamed of rebuilding the village.

"All dreams begin with one person," he said to himself. The Master had told him of his solitary ancestor who had migrated from the Indus river valley thousands of years ago and come to Deccan to be the odd man out—a Brahman Prince; an Aryan among Dravidians.

Thimma named the area Srinivas Nagar after the old Master. He put up a sign to indicate that this was now a new, one-family village.

Still the untouchables were not satisfied.

When the Master returned from Hyderabad, on his next vacation, they went to him directly in a delegation. They told him exactly what had happened.

The Master's short temper began to work again. His rage knew no bounds.

He pulled away Thimma's ragged turban. Then he slapped Thimma on the face. Very hard. And he shouted.

"You bastard, you damned bastard! How dare you not protect your own bed? What good is your intelligence, your wisdom, your reading of the epics if you tend to other people's gardens while your own abounds in *repulsive* weeds? You sing in my *Divan-e-Khas* while your house burns! Your problem is a seed of danger that will burst forth like a thousand-headed cobra and consume us all!"

Thimma listened in silence. Sorrowful silence. He was too full of emotion to do what he was best at doing—finding the right word for the right time at the right place. His bed had been left unprotected for so long, so many years, because of his devotion to the family—the family of Brahman rulers. Night and day he had served them; but his serving had not been without self-interest, had it?

He was peaceful. And humble.

He spoke again. "I am sorry, Master, I was the cause of such pain to you."

The Master was conciliatory. Sad.

"I am sorry too, son! I am sorry I exploded like that with you. You! I am sorry about the whole matter. You want me to do something about it? You want me to conduct a hearing? Punish the bastard? What do you want me to do? If it was somebody else I would have asked for your counsel. Something must be done."

"No, Master. Nothing needs to be done. If you have any compassion, any love for me, leave the matter alone. If all the service I have rendered to you means anything to you, do me, give me, one single favor. Let this be on me. I must settle this all by myself in the best way I can. I must resolve it singly in a way I think is right. Let this be on my honor and my conscience. The favor I ask is you leave me alone."

"But can you live as such an outcast from even the outcasts?"

"I've always been that, Master! When I came to work for you they isolated me because they thought I was trying to be too smart in associating myself so closely with a Brahman. No one has ever accepted me. So? So, I am not going to die. I'll live!"

"Can you live with that animal's child in your wife's womb? And later on your porch?"

"Master, as you taught me once before, in every punishment there is a reward. All sin and degradation must finally bring forth good and virtue in this world, should they not? Isn't that what the scriptures say? Do we not know that the lotus comes out of the mire and mud of the monsoon-filled Deccan ponds? I'll not hurt that child, Master. It's a human being yet to come."

Thimma was driving him crazy as Gandhi had driven him crazy in his youth, with impossible moral dreams. The Master smiled sadly.

"I haven't forgotten that you explained the meaning of *Ramayana* to your own father! But still! Can you burn that revenge out of you? Can you do that? Go home, at least for tonight. Good-night, son!"

Thimma took the familiar road.

Ember shadows. The bleak, arid Deccan plateau stretched in front of him.

Part Five

15

sons

THEY BOTH WENT TO THE ONE-ROOM school that flourished in the villages, off and on, its survival dependent on the goodwill of the peasants and the paucity or plenty of monsoon rains. Neither one of them did well at school. They were both fieldhands and they knew it, as did their parents. Before they were eleven years old they had begun to work on the farms. They knew how to burp the bullocks. They knew how to seed tobacco. They knew how to count sticks of corn and how to measure grain. They knew how to organize the harvest in hundreds of bundles all over the fields.

They were both named after the monkey god, the follower of Rama, Hanuman.

Thimma's son Hanumantha was tough. He learned to drink *tadi* at age twelve. Most of the time he was drunk at a bamboo bar on the outskirts of the railway station town. He was arrogant and he was wild. Thimma wanted the Master to tell him how to curb the boy's wildness. The boy had a hard time even bowing or saluting before the old Master and his family, obsequies which had become merely courtesies now. He stood sullenly most of the time, acting as if he did not know what he was doing wrong.

The Master suggested that Thimma find a nice girl for him and get him married. That was an archetypical Deccan prescription for all problems; marriage. Family responsibility might curb the wildness, the stubbornness and the meanness in the boy.

From among his many distant cousins Thimma found a girl. His Hanumantha was married. The girl was twelve.

Hanumantha's wife was shy, introspective, ordinary-looking, dark and dutiful. She respected her mother-in-law, Ganga, and she never got in Ganga's way. She respected and loved her father-in-law, Thimma, and served him with devotion. She took care of her little brothers-in-law who were not much younger than she was. And she loved her baby sister-in-law, Rangi.

When Marya learned that Thimma had found a bride for his Hanumantha he wanted to find a bride posthaste for his own Hanumantha. Many times Thimma's Hanumantha had bested Marya's Hanumantha, in almost all things. The most important contest had occurred at the pre-monsoon Saint's festival when Thimma's Hanumantha had lifted twice as many stones as Marya's Hanumantha and climbed the grease pole faster than anyone else. Police Marya had tried in vain to get Thimma's son disqualified from the contest on the grounds that he was an untouchable and would thus "contaminate" everything and everybody he touched. The others had balked at this invocation of tradition, but Thimma's Hanumantha, in his drunken, arrogant and bewildering way, had challenged everyone at the festival. He said that the only reason *they* would not let him participate in the festival sports was not because he was a Harijan—an untouchable—but because *they* knew that he was a better athlete than any of *them* and hence superior to *them*. *They* could not face that fact. *They* certainly could not accept the fact that *they* might be defeated and trounced by— of all the people—a Harijan.

Using his inimitable language, Thimma's Hanumantha had cried out: "No man here, touchable or untouchable, has as big and as firm and as powerful a cunt-fucking engine as I do! And you don't like it!"

Police Marya had jumped from his seat and lunged at the Harijan boy. People attempted to restrain Police Marya. Thimma's Hanumantha shouted: "See, you must eat and you must be eaten by your own traditions! You cannot hit me, Marya, and you cannot touch me! I'm *untouchable!* If you touch me you'll lose your caste!" And then Hanumantha laughed wildly, drunkenly, exuberantly.

The elders permitted Hanumantha, the Harijan boy, to enter the contest because no one there wanted to feel that he was unfair and cowardly. The chief of the elders said, "Certainly one has to find out if a touchable can lose to an untouchable in a fair contest. The time has come."

They found out.

Hanumantha, stone-drunk on *tadi*, wild, maniacal and almost superhuman, trounced all his opponents in every contest. When he won his last contest, Hanumantha passed out in a berserk, exultant, alcoholic stupor, clutching at the greased pole near the main platform.

That stung Police Marya to the core. It brought him to the courtyard of Hanuman, the monkey-god's temple.

"Twenty-years ago it was not any worthless *Harijan* who won all the contests," Marya railed. "It was Police Marya. It was Marya who was declared the undisputed champion of Kusumurthy and indeed of all of Gudur-upon-Bhima. It was his physical prowess that established his authority as the police patel of the village."

Now that ancestral position was in jeopardy.

Marya felt quite sorry for his own son, Hanumantha alias Mallik.

"He has lost all the contests in the very first rounds," Marya wailed. "My Hanumantha will never be a champion. He is mild and he is growing milder by the day. Most of the time he just sits in the barn, feeding hay to the cattle and playing his crude reed. Occasionally he walks the fields of Kusumurthy on lonely moonlit nights. When people insult him he ignores them. And to add insult to injury, he says he has been reading a book of Gandhi that he has borrowed from Sali Thimma—of all people."

The villagers called Marya's son Mallik for his mildness, after a Moghul white flower of the Deccan. His official name, Hanumantha, was only for the records.

"I want something to be done," Police Marya said. "Something that will wash away all the humiliations of the recent past. I beg you, Thimma! Please use your influence with the great Master to arrange for a loan. Five thousand rupees will be sufficient."

"No! Absolutely not." Thimma said. "You have not repaid a single debt so far."

Marya was furious.

He went to the Master's rivals across the river and made all kinds of promises to them about helping establish their economic power in the villages this side of the river. Even as he made the promises, Marya knew full well that he would be in no position to keep them. But that did not deter him.

"What was at stake was my honor, my pride," he told Thimma on his return to the village.

"The very same thing for which nations and potentates have waged wars, killed millions, and become insolvent down through the centuries."

"Your problem is, Thimma, you are always thinking of the

past or the future. I have to live very much in the present. Do you understand?"

"Quite well, unfortunately."

After he signed hundreds of papers for them, the rich people across the river lent Marya enormous amounts of money.

Marya celebrated his son's wedding in grand style. The girl was beautiful, well-shaped and quite lascivious. Marya said, "If she were not the bride of my son, I would have fucked her myself, so beautiful she is!" Marya invited members of all the four castes to the wedding feasts. Marya even invited the old Master.

"Of course, I will not attend!" the Master said. "But I'll make a concession to such a festive occasion." He called the little Prince to the *Diwan-e-Khas*.

"You represent me at the wedding," the Master told Vishnoo. "You're going to have to live with the younger generation, so you'd better get to know them as well as you can."

For nine days each caste was served at a different time and a different place. Marya served sixteen prime lambs, three hundred thirty-six chickens, twenty sacks of white, yellow and brown rice, and mounds of sweets made with cardamom and cloves and first-class butter. In daily life Marya would never eat all these foods in such a lavish and extravagant way. Or serve them. "This is a feast to end all feasts, the blast of my life," said Marya. "This will show Thimma who is superior."

Marya went broke. He had mortgaged all his earnings for the next ten years. The only thing left for him to do was to bully the villagers into subsidizing his living.

16
hiatus

WHEN THEY WERE SIXTEEN, both of them caught a dreadful disease. They became thin and emaciated as the days passed by. They could not eat any food. Not much anyway.

Thimma took his son to the doctor at the railway station.

"It's the wasting disease," the doctor told Thimma. "You will have to take your son to the sanitarium located in the hills of Vikarabad. Maybe the air of the hills can cure him. I don't know."

"I am not about to take any chances, Doctor Sahib. I am boarding the next train to Vikarabad."

He literally had to carry his son on board the train. Young Hanumantha had a very hard time breathing and walking simultaneously.

At the sanitarium Thimma begged the doctors, "Please! You must save my son, no matter what the cost. I will sell my last sheepswool blanket, and even the Master's crops if it comes to that. I am a Harijan—an untouchable. The country and the doctors owe it to me, if they believe one ounce in the teachings of the Mahatma. You doctors here owe it to me if you believe one ounce in your conscience."

Doctor Gurudwar told Thimma, "Things have changed a lot more than you think or give credit for. *We* don't have to do you any favors, anything special at all. It's already been done in the constitution drafted by the great untouchable, Dr. Ambedkar. Since you are a member of the scheduled castes, there are indeed some special facilities the government has made available for you and your family at the sanitarium."

Thimma left Young Hanumantha in a sparse clinical room overlooking the barren dry hills and valleys of Vikarabad, and he returned to Kusumurthy.

Police Marya frowned on what Sali Thimma had done. Marya

cursed the government for offering special facilities to the untouchables.

"I cannot follow the same course as an untouchable!" he raved. "My own son Hanumantha, alias Mallik, is made of better mettle. He's from a higher caste. He will recover on his own. He doesn't need no damned government-appointed doctor!"

Marya went to the barn and patted Mallik strongly on the back. The young fellow grimaced in pain.

As the villagers said, Marya's Mallik had "caught the bed" for several weeks now. He was wasting away. Mallik did not go to the fields anymore. Even his cattle became emaciated for lack of daily care. One bull died of eating excessively of the crushed corn.

"He'll come through, he'll come through," thundered Marya all over the village.

"I don't think I will, I don't think I will," Mallik said to himself.

Mallik's bride remained with the family. She did not have any particular interest in the housekeeping chores. And Marya did not want to let her go to the fields. "She even makes the bulls' cocks stand up," he shouted.

In India each village has a temple at its gates. That is the temple of the monkey god, Hanuman. Hanuman protects the villagers from any harm.

Mallik's bride went to the temple of Hanuman by the huge tree and played checkers with other village girls.

17

revelation

THIMMA'S HANUMANTHA RETURNED from the sanitarium in six months. He was looking extremely well. Thimma was proud of his son. There was no *tadi* in the sanitarium, so even Hanumantha's manners were improved.

Thimma paraded his son all over the village. "Oh! What the government is doing for untouchables!" Thimma cried in gratitude.

Marya refused to acknowledge Hanumantha's existence.

Hanumantha went back to the farm.

One day Thimma took him to his father's grave. There they sat on the bluff and stared solemnly at the river.

"I wonder if it purifies us, son, this great mother, our river? I wonder if it cleanses stains, wounds that seem to remain painful as ever, even as they heal on the outside? A terrible wrong was done to me—to our family—on this very ground where your grandfather is buried."

"I know, father, I know."

"You know?"

"What do you think I am? A fool? Why do you think I took to drinking? One night I had a butcher's knife and I wanted to cut that whore's throat with it."

Thimma slapped his son hard on the face. "You disrespectful scoundrel! How dare you talk of your mother like that?"

"I don't give a damn about your authority and your force and your power. What the hell happened to them all when *she* was sleeping with that low-down bastard in the village? He was not even an untouchable! She's a whore and you better accept that fact, wise man! And don't, don't ever call *her* my mother!"

Thimma's face streamed with tears. "You too, son! You want me to accept that? Okay, I will! I'm a cuckold! I am low! I am powerless! I am naked! I am a worthless human being. Are you happy now?"

Hanumantha froze in deep mortification. It was not in him to apologize.

18

seduction

HANUMANTHA WAS ON THE PROWL. He looked at the fields that Police Marya owned. They were desolate. Hanumantha would have attempted to attack any bullock carts that Marya might have had. But they were all in hock to the loansharks who had provided the money for the grand wedding. There were no contests in which he could vanquish Marya's son, Mallik. Hanumantha roamed and roamed the countryside, trying to come up with some desperate plan.

His eyes lighted upon the temple at the gates to the village —the temple of Hanuman—the god after whom both he and Marya's son had been named.

She sat on the high platform, the thirty brass and iron bells pealing gently because of the blowing hot, dry, summer wind. There was no one to play checkers with her today. She was just throwing pieces at random and playing with her pretty black hair in exhausted boredom. Boredom was a universal and perpetual disease in the Deccan. People did not want to do anything, but they always complained of having nothing to do.

Hanumantha knew he was not supposed to enter the temple. If Police Marya's people saw him he would be finished.

Hanumantha raised his dhoti and tied it up high so that she could see his long legs. Then he straightened his *rumal*—his turban—and cocked it at a rakish angle.

"Someone wants you at the farm near the river bend!"

She looked up. She knew who he was. She attributed almost superhuman qualities to him. He had recovered from a disease that was wasting away her husband, Mallik. Hanumantha looked strong and vigorous. His dark brown body gleamed in the sun. No Harijan had spoken to her in that manner before.

"Who wants me?" she asked mischievously. "You know quite well that no one wants me. At least no one you would know!"

"Someone wants you, God damn it. If you don't go up to the river now this someone is going to be hopping mad!"

"You lead the way, untouchable man, and you make sure I am well protected. I have never been in the untouchables' fields before."

He walked ahead of her. He found the most desolate lonely little footpaths in the fields that were not yet harvested. She followed him, clutching her jewelry so it would not jangle. They went by the backroads. The more tantalized and anxious she was, the more Hanumantha delayed her approach to his grandfather's grave. "The village must be robbed," he said to himself.

He took her through the low summer river. They hopped and skipped and jumped over the red, black, asphalt-grey and white rocks. They walked through the dry mud by the river bank.

Finally they arrived at his grandfather's grave. Behind the hay, he stood and surveyed the farm.

"Who wants me here?" she said, playing with a dry, golden corn stick.

"I do. I want you, you goddamned sugarcane-cutting, sugar cunt, upper-caste golden ass, I want you!"

"Are you crazy, you goddamned, low-class, low-caste, low-lying untouchable? Son of an untouchable whore. You can't touch me!"

"But my cock can!" And with that, in absolute savagery, Hanumantha dragged her down into the hay, and pulled away her handloomed saree and unbuttoned her scant checkered green blouse. She pushed him away with all the strength she could muster. But every inch of resistance was only a challenge to him —to his passion which had been rekindled intensely since he had recovered from the wasting disease. He was lithe; charged with all the dry energy he had absorbed in the dry hills of Vikarabad.

19

rebel

I T WAS THE MONSOON SEASON. But no rain was in sight. The summer crops had been harvested and marketed in the hiatus of June. There was not much to do except to wait anxiously for the Deccan farms to be fortunate.

In the evening, praying for rain, all the villagers gathered at the village temple and the Brahman priest with the thin, narrow face and the round, clean-shaven head narrated tales from the *Ramayana,* the *Mahabharata* and the *Panchatantra.* The Brahman narrated the tales; the merchants supplied the coconuts, the oil for the wicker candles and the dry popcorn; the Harijans swept the ground; and the others made their own contribution in cash or kind. But the only thought on everyone's mind was of rain. Rain must come. They asked the Brahman to intercede and offer prayers to Indra, the god of gods—the god of rain; and to Varuna, the god of water and clouds.

At one of the prayer meetings, Thimma approached Marya.

"I think that little boy of yours, gentle Mallik, is wasting away. Why don't you take him to the railway station and check with the doctor? Maybe someone there can give you a loan to take the kid to the hospital. Don't you see how well my Hanumantha has recovered?"

Police Marya pounced on Thimma. "Oh, you low-class, low, mean, dirty, conniving, untouchable bastard! You've taken away his bride! And now you want to insult his father by telling him what to do about his own son?"

"Two men behaved as animals. You and my son. But still I am sorry. If I had not been so busy with Master's work, maybe I could have prevented it. I don't know. With my Hanumantha I can never be sure of anything. He is as much of an animal now as you were ten years ago!"

"How dare you compare me with your filthy, rotten little casteless mongrel, you goddamned untouchable? How dare you?"

"I said I'm sorry, even though I am not directly responsible for all this. But the only thing about being sorry is that you cannot really undo the wrong done."

"Damn right, you can't. But I'll find a way to serve justice. I'll destroy all you goddamned untouchables until there is no trace of any one of you in this countryside. Yah! I'll cut your cocks!"

The next day Marya set about organizing his caste to attack the Harijans. He did not tell anybody why he wanted to attack them.

Learning of Marya's plans, Thimma's Hanumantha got himself together. His own brother, Bhima, had left for Hyderabad to be trained and employed by the Allwyn Metal Works as a security officer. But there were several other unemployed, uneducated Harijan kids around, kids his age and younger. Hanumantha was not going to involve any member of the older generation.

"All the old ones are dickless bastards who never stood up to anything," Hanumantha announced to the young untouchables. He was a leader. "Yes, old means dickless in the Deccan. But untouchable is not going to mean that anymore. Harijan is not going to mean that anymore. Hanumantha is going to change all that. From now on the word Harijan will stand for fear. Yes, the others are going to shit in their upper-caste dhotis whenever a Harijan boy walks by. Yes, Hanumantha is going to get every ax, pick, knife, old sword, club and *bandook* available for you."

"God! I wish it would rain," Thimma cried, and prayed at the temple at the village gate. He attempted to talk to his son and counsel him.

"Counsel me? You old fool! Let me counsel you as you used to counsel your father! A Harijan neither gives nor takes counsel, I say. That's a goddamned Brahman thing to do, which might make us lose *our* caste. You, my father, you are a bastard. You are a sheep in a tiger's skin. You are a Brahman in a Harijan body. That's why you are so afraid of action. God damn it, you will not manipulate me anymore. And you will not manipulate the village with your cunning and cowardly lies. Your politicking in the village to keep peace is not going to work. Up to now we untouchables were accustomed to taking orders. Now we are going to give some!"

20

solution

THE YOUNG ONES FROM THE MIDDLE castes had all left the village to work in the factories of Bombay, the restaurants of Poona, the cafes of Bangalore and the government offices of Hyderabad. They preferred to live in the slums of the cities where, even if their homes did not have electricity, there was always a chance, an opportunity for them to walk under the electrified streetlights and eat in well-lit restaurants. Back home it was all lonely darkness and an endless wait for the monsoon.

The only young ones left in Kusumurthy were Marya's own children, four of them: the oldest son, Mallik, gentle and weak and wasting away; the others too little and too young to count. But Marya organized all the grey-haired men. In Indian villages most villagers had grey hair before they were fifty. None of them was in any condition to fight the young, virile and wild Harijan boys. But Marya exhorted them in the name of the family, communal honor and ancestry.

Thimma knew he had to talk. He had been totally ostracized by the young untouchables. He was hoping against hope that the older ones among the cane-gatherers would listen to reason. He knew that pressure, direct and invisible, was an important force in reasoning.

When Thimma approached Marya, who was sitting under the huge banyan tree twirling his greying moustache, Marya jumped like a ferocious tiger and slapped him.

"I have done it!" he shouted. "I've done it! Finally I hit an untouchable with my own hands! Now I can hit the others!"

"No, you can't. I'll let this pass. You've insulted me in worse ways. But listen to me now! You cannot fight the young ones. They are strong; and they are ruthless! You have no young men to fight for you. Your other children are twelve, nine and seven. My God, man, think of your own survival!"

"Get out of my sight, get out of my sight, you cunning bastard! Your mind is poisoned with intelligence!"

Thimma laughed at the irony of the remark, and Marya thought Thimma was insulting him again. He brandished his old brown club. Thimma walked away.

Thimma went to each and every one of Marya's relatives. He explained the situation to them.

The cane-gatherers, loathing Thimma as they did, yet listened to him. They knew that Thimma—Sali Thimma, Schoolman-Untouchable—had the cunning of a fox and the compassion of a god. Stealthily, at night, Thimma showed them the amassed arsenal of weapons in the Harijan quarter. He told them that if they did not strike the first blow, he would see to it that the Harijan boys did not strike a single blow either.

The cane-gatherers withdrew their support for Police Marya. Marya thundered and declaimed that he would kill all the Harijans, singly. The cane-gatherers knew they did not have the strength to fight all the young, rowdy ones, but they had enough strength to sequester Marya and lock him up for a few days. They knew they had done this for Marya's own good.

Thimma argued with the Harijan boys. They told him not to talk to them. He said he was going to, no matter what happened.

"I am telling you for the last time! Whatever your pride, if they do not strike the first blow, they are admitting they are not in a position to attack. So they are acknowledging to you that you are strong. And even after that, if you attack them, I'll have no recourse but to come and chop your heads off. Yes! I mean that. I'll start with my own son. I have given everything I had to bring him back to health, to give him a second life. Now I'll give everything I have to save your lives and theirs. If you go against my orders (and believe me, they are orders!), you know how cunning and low and scheming and deceiving I am! Like the Deccan devil I'll come in the middle of the night and cut your throats. And then I won't care what happens to me. I am an old man. If they take me to jail, I'll read the *Ramayana* and meditate. The great godlike man, my hero, Gandhi, did that. The Master did that. You have heard of the cunning and deceitful Thimma, haven't you? That's me!" His eyes were livid with rage. "You just don't know what I am capable of!"

They really did not know what Thimma was capable of. They

did not know how Thimma had managed to study all those books about different countries and different times, living in such a small village in the desolate Deccan. They did not know how Thimma had become so close to a Brahman master. They did not know how Thimma had come to live with himself after his own wife had been first raped and then seduced by Marya, who had let the whole countryside know about it. That required some inexplicable wisdom or courage or both. They did not know why Thimma wanted to save the life of the man who had harmed him most. They did not understand such strange compassion. They did not know how and where Thimma had found the resources to get his son admitted to the hospital. There was always something unfathomable about Thimma!

They realized, recognized that they were genuinely afraid of Thimma, of the unknown factor in him. Thimma represented what was not predictable and therein lay his power.

Without declaring so, they backed down. They reasoned, "As long as we are not attacked first, we are still the victors!"

21

extinction

ONE DAY, POLICE MARYA WENT to the small city of Raichur to see the latest Hindi movie that had been released. His favorite actress, Hema Malini, was starring in it.

While Marya was gone, his son Mallik got worse. He began to wheeze and cough without respite. He panted in indescribable pain. The children became afraid. The women in the house went wild with fear and anxiety. "Can someone get the doctor at the railway station, oh God, can someone?" the mother cried.

Marya's second oldest son, Rama, knew he had to do something. He harnessed the neighbor's cart. His little brother, Mallanna III, and his little sister, Lalitha, jumped into the cart with Rama. The little girl, out of sheer nervousness, ogled her older brother, and played little word games with him. They sped towards the railway station. They came to the railway crossing separating the state of Andhra Pradesh from the state of Karnataka. The crossing guard had shut the gate and gone to town for lunch. They waited an hour. He was still not back.

Rama said: "Let us cross the track beyond the culvert. I don't think anything will hurt us."

As Rama herded the bulls over the railroad tracks, the distant sound of the modern Bombay-Madras express could be heard. It became louder by the second. The bulls became terrified and paralyzed. They refused to budge. The cart wheels were stuck in the stone pellets spread over the railroad track to give it traction and stability. The children cried and shrieked. The bulls bellowed agonizingly. The train smashed them.

The doctor arrived for the police autopsy.

22

temple

THAT EVENING POLICE MARYA returned from Raichur. He wanted to tell his family all about Hema Malini and her movie. Watching movies was the most important Indian national pastime.

Mallik lay dead on the rope cot in the barn. His reed lay next to him.

The women had surrounded the body. "Oh God! I wish the doctor was here. And the other children. Or at least the monsoon. So all of us could be washed away," cried the boy's mother.

Marya cried, "Oh no! He can't die! Not so young! We Police Patels can't die. Who'll collect the criminal's tax after I am gone? He must live. What has happened to his will? His grandfather lived to be one hundred and three! Nothing rubbed off on Mallik! Nothing! None of our heredity! Oh, my God! What is the worst thing that can happen to a man? When he has to bury his own child! That is putting the cart before the bullocks, God!" Marya wept.

Next morning, the state police van arrived from the railway station. It contained the bodies of Rama, Mallanna III and Lalitha.

Marya went to Hanuman's temple at the village gates. He kicked the red door of the inner sanctum.

"You, goddamn, mother-fucking God, you! Who the hell do you protect on this Deccan plain? Do you ever listen to me? Why did you take your revenge on my children, you goddamned fucker? They were not responsible for my sins! Take me away! They say Emperor Babar gave his life and brought his son, Humayun, back to earth. They say the Master's mother, the old dowager, died so he could live. Take me away, God! But please, bring back Mallik! Bring back Rama, Lalitha and Mallanna III!" And Marya rang the bells hanging from the ceiling, furiously, one after another.

A week later, Police Marya went to the Mansion. He wanted to see the Master.

Marya was admitted immediately.

He prostrated himself before the Master and his turban touched the Master's feet.

"I know not where to turn, Master. There is no living God in the Deccan. You are as near to God as I can see around here. Thimma has been the lucky one. He has worshipped you and loved you and he has been rewarded with everything. I've been afraid of you and I've tried to run away. It's my forefathers' sins that are being visited upon me, Master. My father paid for your father to be killed. And I seduced Thimma's wife. It is retribution. I am being punished. I am lonely and I am disconsolate. There is not a single grain, bird, animal, man, woman or temple that consoles me today in the Deccan. I am lost, Master, I am lost! Even as I repent I cannot be forgiven."

The Master lifted Marya up and he hugged him closely. His eyes streamed with tears for the bereaved man.

"No one can forgive anyone in this world, son! I doubt God plans the tragedies that take place so meaninglessly in our lives. Time has passed by us like the river Bhima. It's forever different, and yet it's the same as it was in your forefathers' times and in my ancestors' times. I do not know the consolation that can bring you out of your grief. The only consolation, if it is a consolation at all, is that we are brothers in sin and in sorrow."

The Master served dinner for Marya with his own hand. Marya knew the Master had never done this. Not even for Thimma. Not even for his own wife.

Part Six

23

monsoon

NEXT YEAR THE MONSOON ARRIVED with a hellish fury.
It rained. The top soil was completely washed away. The
river flooded. It drowned the Saint's shrine on its banks. The
streams and the creeks and the artesian wells in the Master's
desolate mango orchard overflowed with mud and muddy water.

The Mansion and its compounds were surrounded on all four
sides by water.

That afternoon the Master went to pray at the temple of
Hanuman. Still at his prayers, he fell to the floor. They rushed up
to him. Vishnoo, the young Prince, lifted him up. The Master could
not speak. He stuttered rapidly.

Vishnoo was stoical. He arranged for bamboo tops to be
floated as rafts over the creek that separated the Mansion from the
railway station.

"There has never been so much water in the mango orchard,"
said Thimma, smiling weakly.

It poured on them as they trekked to the railway station.
Through the pigeonhole of the cart, the Master stared vacuously at
all the land around him. He could hardly see it. He tried to talk
to everyone around him. No one understood him.

They reached the railway station.

The doctor came to the first-class waiting room and adminis-
tered a shot. "His condition is very serious," he told Vishnoo. "He
has had a very severe stroke. All the stress, pressure and pain of
taking care of so many people, such a vast land, has finally gotten
to him. You must take him to Hyderabad tonight."

The lamps emitted dim light at the railway station. The young
Prince lifted the Master in his arms and boarded the train.

As the train left, the retinue saluted. "I am sure he will be
all right, little Prince," said Thimma in parting.

The train reached the hill station of Vikarabad at two a.m. The
Master had passed away.

24

havoc

T HE WATERS SUBSIDED. THE COUNTRYSIDE dried up as quickly as it had flooded. They brought the Master back to the villages. The fair-complexioned priest with the dark, shining, piercing, mesmerizing eyes, who had shaved his head clean and who wore nothing but a sacred thread and an orange silk dhoti, chanted passages from the Rig Veda; passages from the Hymn of Creation, Agni and Soma; passages incantatory, invocatory and reverberating in the stillness of the third floor rooms of the Mansion:

"Non-being then existed not, nor being:
There was no air, nor sky that is beyond it.
What was concealed? Wherein? In whose protection?
And was there deep unfathomable water?

Death then existed not, nor life immortal;
Of neither night nor day was any token.
By its inherent force the One breathed windless;
No other thing than that beyond existed.

Darkness there was at first, by darkness hidden;
Without distinctive marks, this all was water.
That which, becoming, by the void was covered,
That One by force of heat came into being.

.   .   .

Thy flames when driven by the wind, O Agni,
Disperse, O pure one, pure in all directions;
And thy divine Navagvas, most destructive,
Lay low the woods and devastate them boldly.

Thy steeds, the bright, the pure, O radiant Agni,
Let loose, speed on and shave the ground beneath them.
Thy whirling flame then widely shines refulgent,
The highest ridges of earth's surface reaching.

When the bull's tongue darts forward like the missile
Discharged by him who fights the cows to capture,
Like hero's onset is the flame of Agni:
Resistless, dreadful, he consumes the forests.

.   .   .

Like fire produced by friction make me brilliant."

Though the Master's family had adopted the Yajur Veda as
their family Veda, the Master himself had had a great personal
preference for the Rig Veda. "The first among the Vedas and the
most poetic," he called it.

The young Prince touched the handsome priest's feet. Prostrated. Wept. The young man needed consolation from the learned
one.

The priest, not much older than the young Prince, was stern,
other-worldly. His power came from his distance from the young
Prince. He commanded the Prince. "Arise, my son! Arise! Listen
and do as the Vedas have commanded us to do for three thousand
years."

The Prince was terrified; afraid of the weight of tradition that
he did not clearly understand or empathize with.

The priest spoke. "You and your brothers must serve the high
priests and the *deevans* (the archbishops of the *mutts*—the
churches) in the inner sanctum of the temple by the river that no
one else can enter. You must bathe in the holy river Bhima; the
reeffulgence and the reincarnation of the Ganga in the Deep South.
Then, with no leather vestiges anywhere in the vicinity—you must
make sure of that—and no human skin ever touching you during
the period, with only a silk shawl and a silk dhoti, with burning
feet touching the scorching earth and disregarding the evergrowing
thorns and the ever-chipping stones by the river, you must come
back from the river, and carry hot rice in dried-palm containers,
accompanied by lentil soup and non-aphrodisiac vegetables such as
spinach and cabbage, and serve the funeral meal which must, in
its spare simplicity, mirror the simple, spare nothingness of death."

The young Prince was crushed. For some time, at least, he did
not want to accept the fact that his father was dead.

The priest continued. "During the Meal, you, being the eldest

son of the Master, must stand all through the prayer ceremonies
and aid your father in reaching heaven by chanting shlokas from
the *Rig Veda,* your father's preferred one. In the order that I was
chanting and invoking this morning, the *shlokas* will begin by
questioning the existence and nature of God; they will conclude by
emphasizing the value and the definite possibility of reincarnation
and continuity, and the inalienable link between this world and the
next, the present and the future. Once these recitations are con-
cluded you must, with the proper attitude, in serene, humble sup-
plication and submission, offer *Dakshina*—the gift of money to the
priests. The greater the scholar or the more powerful the priest, the
higher must be his *Dakshina.* And then, accepting little portions
of food from all the priests' plates, you must sprinkle them, a grain
at a time, on the plates of all come for the Meal. The sprinkling
will make those plates twice-blessed. Thus you will *begin* the Meal
for the secular mourners of all castes. Outside the temple. On the
beautiful, dark Deccan earth. On banana leaves.

"Even there; even outside the temple do not forget order,
hierarchy, system, plan. Do not invite chaos and thereafter annihi-
lation. Respect the nature of evolution."

"Why do you say that to me? Are you afraid that I am a
heathen?"

"No, but people trained in a way different from the ancient
one might not know why all this was fashioned. Please remember.
First the secular Brahmans, those who are Brahmans by birth only
and not by training, must be served. Then the members of the
warrior caste of whom there are not many left in your villages, even
though many lay claim, without credentials, to that caste."

The Prince knew the rest even though the priest did not think
he did. After the warrior caste the trader caste must be served, the
trader caste with all its sub-castes, the people who did not indulge
in any meat-eating or alcohol drinking. Their only venality—if it
could be considered that at all—was the precious accumulation and
distribution of money. They had made even that into a chaste,
clean, vegetarian art whereby most of them seemed not to have
been tainted by Mammon. They performed the most essential functions of society. Even the food for today's funeral rites was there
because this caste had been able philosophically to comprehend
and use the principles of production, distribution and acquisition
as community tools. Mahatma Gandhi belonged to this caste.

Then came the fourth caste, sometimes called the fourth people, and divided into hundreds of sub-castes. People such as Police
Marya and Badyala Hanumantha Rao and Jimkala Mallanna belonged to this caste: people who had mixed or changed castes and
people whose professions had once marked them as only physical
beings. But now they were rising far above the earth, politically and
economically.

Below and beyond all the castes were the untouchables who
never had been asked until now if they ever wanted to mix and
mingle and become one with the rest of the world. The untouchables were the ones who could eat meat at all times. And the
untouchables were the majority of the Indians. They were non-
vegetarians by desire and vegetarians by necessity. Often they told
each other that a traditional Brahman religious meal was almost
always like a funeral meal, no matter what the occasion—so sparse
and meatless it was!

The priest said, "I expect everything to proceed in a proper
manner. As the eldest son you are responsible for being stoic,
determined, responsible and dignified. Anything that goes wrong
will be at your door. You have inherited your father's place. Remember that. Do not do anything foolish or self-destructive. I will
see you at the river."

The Prince was all alone. He seethed. "No matter what their
instincts tell them, no one wants the caste system to be truly broken
down because there still is the deep-seated fear and trust of religion
in them, the fear and trust that prevents them from being free, the
fear and trust that has helped theology and social law to mix so
inalienably in this ancient nation of mine. In India, as in the rest
of this part of the world, the religious and the social law are one
and the same. The goodness and the deep corruption of our soci-
eties spring from this source. It makes us noble and inward-looking
at the same time. Without question and without respite."

The Prince was agitated. Unhappy. Something had to be done.

In the distance, sandalwood and tamarind wood, thorns and
pine needles were slowly being gathered into a platform. Soon the
old Master would ascend to heaven.

The Master had asked that his ashes be scattered in the Bhima
River to become once again a part of the deep Deccan earth from
which he had sprung and which he loved so much. The young
Prince knew that as the ashes flowed downstream towards the Bay

of Bengal into the interminable East, the traditions, the values and the systems which had made his father's life what it was would disappear forever with them; with him. There would not be a single structure from the Master's plan that would be preserved in a world that had changed so dramatically, so rapidly and so unbelievably.

The young man invited every living man and woman within the vast range of the countryside, the area in between the three rivers, to come and pay respects to his father. Every person from every caste was invited. Brahman, Warrior, Trader, The Fourth Man and The Untouchable. In telling them that they were free to do what they wanted and go wherever they pleased; in telling them that each one of them could come and literally *touch* the old Master's feet and light a sandalwood stick at his pyre, the Prince was bringing down the house of order. He made a private ceremony into a public one; and now there was no telling what this would lead to.

As much as they had despised Thimma in the past for hopping and skipping along caste borders, no matter how subtly and sensitively he did it, the villagers' dislike of Thimma was nothing compared with what they felt for the Prince now. Startled by this unexpected and for some of them very much unwanted intimacy with the body, life and death of a Brahman, they were still intrigued and physically pleased at the thought of being so totally free; of being allowed to touch what they were never supposed to touch. Even as they cursed and abused the Prince in their private, hush-hush gossip sessions, they prepared with excitement to meet their newfound freedoms and privileges.

All except Thimma.

Thimma was not pleased. He knew what the young Master wanted. But he also realized in a shock of recognition what the young Master had so suddenly and so totally given up. By what he had done, the young man had given up authority. He had given up, without realizing, the responsibility and the privilege of being the father of the whole group of villages; of being the Master.

In that man who was slowly ascending to heaven that evening, in that holy flame that consumed his body, the old world—of patriarchy and collective responsibility, the old, larger world of socially interdependent village families—was dead.

The Prince, the young Prince, with the same kind of idealism that had burned in Thimma secretly for years, would soon be condemned to live in the modern Indian purgatory of nothingness; of alienation, and of chaos. Without the intricate hierarchical structure that the Master had developed and preserved to feed the people, albeit in a meager way, the Prince would not be able to provide food for them. And without food there could be no Prince. The democratic Prince who did not want to order anyone about in the old way would not be able to answer the needs of six thousand, six hundred thousand, and eventually six hundred sixty-six million people. The Prince wanted a complete change. But neither he nor the world had produced the mechanism which would help one-fifth of its population make the rapid leap. Thus were purgatories born, dark and empty and unavoidable. Where should one turn? Both the past and the future were equally distant.

And Thimma?

"I will be what I have never been before. A betrayer. I will never be able to keep the promise to the Master, the promise of helping his son to carry on. Betrayal is implicit in the transformation that will take place this very dark afternoon, heaven help me! I will betray the old Master on the day of his funeral without ever wanting to do so. Dear Master! You! You, the great canopy who covered all of us—villages, castes, traditions and little hopes— within your vast reaches, you have flown off. The Deccan is naked. And now there is only the vast nude sky of India, clear and bright and cloudless and scorching and pitiless, asking us to see ourselves clearly without pity, without compassion, without the comforting darkness of the past. There is no shelter, no Master anywhere in sight. And the young Master needs *me.*"

Thimma would betray the Master. And so would the Prince, the young man, the Prince who did not want to be a Prince anymore. He would betray his father, his family and his traditions. His education, his international growing up, his need for rapid change and immediate results made it so very difficult (oh yes, so very difficult for the poor, uncompromising young man—Thimma felt great compassion for the Prince and his dilemmas; tears streamed down his cheeks thinking of the young Master, so bereft of father and faith in the old and the slow) for him to accept things as they were forever and ever more. His life, his time, his destiny and his karma would make it impossible for him to build an organization, a structure, a system that could take slow root and grow and spread itself and eventually nourish others. To do that in modern times would be an invitation to economic and social suicide. The Prince would become a victim of the predestination that determined his being born in the middle of the twentieth century.

The present would become the past even as one barely touched it.

And the future?

The future would elude everyone as bitingly and chillingly as a cold mirage on a dry Deccan winter day that tantalizes the traveler with hazy reflections even as every forward step confirms only the gradual enveloping darkness.

Thimma looked at the Prince. The innocent young man was standing at a distance from the pyre near the river, staring at the gathering clouds and the threatening rain and his slowly disappearing father.

Thimma recollected an old poem he had composed in his youth. It was about doomsday.

Trees will be uprooted,
land will dry
and no arteries
will connect the waterwells.
And then the people of Deccan
will walk the burning land,
barefoot and restless
and scorched.
Revolution will be here
masquerading as transformation.

25

naked in deccan

T HE RAIN NEVER CAME.

Clouds appeared and disappeared constantly. Finally the river glistened in the late afternoon sun. It was time for the great funeral meal that the fair-complexioned priest with the mesmerizing eyes had described.

Chants and supplications. Scorching feet. River that will carry *him* down away from the young man. Life—equality of people— must emerge now. HE would have wanted it, even if he did not want to do that himself. But the time had come. His death had to be a time of rebirth, a time for the reincarnation of India. His fundamental instincts for change with justice should find its flowering on the day of his ascending to heaven. A floral offering, dear father.

Dressed in a dark red shawl and a pure white silk dhoti, the Prince appeared on the scene.

"I will not serve anyone in the inner sanctum!" he cried. "Like fire produced by friction, make me brilliant. Let me shine for all of you. Let us shine together."

The headman of the trader caste, the man who owned the central store in Kusumurthy, Storeman Nagayya, whispered anxiously. "The boy is grief-stricken beyond rational belief!"

The Prince addressed the priests inside the temple now.

"Let me ring the bells. Let me invoke my father to bring us together! The Brahmans and the Untouchables. The Untouchables and all other castes. Let castes mean individuality not separation. I will not serve people separately anymore. Priests, warriors, traders, fourth people, untouchables—and if there is a sixth caste that I don't know about—let me touch all of you now. All at the same time. Let me touch you. And let me be touched by you. Let me serve you this simple food. Nothing but simple cabbages and spinach here. From now on I'm not a Master. I am a servant of the people."

Outside, Thimma heard the Prince. "Oh, God!" he cried.

From inside, the chief priest of the temple, the father of the fair-complexioned priest with the mesmerizing eyes, said, "Are you finished, young man?"

"You, sir, great religious leader, learned man! Let your learned companion, your learned son, touch us all.

When the bull's tongue darts forward like the missile
Discharged by him who fights the cows to capture,
Like hero's onset is the flame of Agni:
Resistless, dreadful, he consumes the forests.

. . .

Like fire produced by friction, make us brilliant, O Brahman!

"Come and serve with me, sir!"

The Prince rang the huge bells tied to the banyan tree in the courtyard of the temple. And he rang the bells of the stone entrance to the inner sanctum and the bells on the rough-hewn redwood pillars of the hall where the Brahman priests were waiting for the funeral meal.

The sounds spread in a multiple cascade of music that flowed on and on into the river full of rocks. And they echoed back.

The priest with the mesmerizing eyes said, "You should not touch the bells overlooking the river in the inner sanctum, young man! You are a secular Brahman!"

"You are not much older than I am, sir! Yes, sir, I am a secular Brahman! I am a secular human being! Like fire produced by friction, make us brilliant, O Brahman! I will not serve; I will not feed the past! I'll serve you, sirs, only if you come out of the temple and sit on the ground. There isn't enough room for all the people of Deccan inside that beautiful but small temple."

"We will have to consider preventing your father's entrance into heaven! He seems to have committed the sin of ill-training you!"

"No, sir, I'll not serve. And I'll not offer each one of you ten rupees apiece. I've nothing but paise in my sack. Each one of you will get a paisa with your meal and so will everyone out there, priest or patel! No more! No more separations between temple and people, between Brahman and Untouchable, between the landlords and the landtiller! I will treat everyone equally. And I will!"

"No one will partake of the meal, young man," the chief priest said. "No one will! And what you are doing will destroy society! And ultimately the world! Will destroy everything your father built! Is that what you want? It will unleash forces you'll never be able to control! A priest is a prophet. Be warned. Even the crow will not come from the southern Ganga to peck at your father's *pinda*. The rice will remain untouched. And he'll obtain neither *Shantih* nor *Moksha!* You'll lock your father forever in this purgatory—this world!"

The temple bells cantillated. Birds flew onto the river Bhima from every direction. Evening approached.

Tying the huge sack of pennies to his dhoti, the Prince went to the outdoor kitchen and lifted a great pail of rice.

Only his brothers followed him. Even his cousins withdrew.

His hands became red with the heat of the boiled, boiling rice. With stoic strength he began serving the banana leaves one by one and offered each one of the diners a paisa.

All remained standing. No one sat down to eat.

Someone from the back shouted.

"Has the Brahman been served?"

"The Brahman is serving!" the Prince shouted back.

There were no banana leaves for the third, fourth and fifth rows. They had simply run out of them. The crowd was far more than anyone had expected. "It seems all of India is here!" Jimkala Mallanna, the treasurer of the Mansion, exclaimed. They would have to resort to dried mango leaves.

The Prince laid all the leaves. Then he served the rice. Lentil soup on top. Cabbage and spinach on the side.

All rows were served. No one was eating. They stared in great tension and silence at the rice and the lentil soup and cabbage and spinach.

"If you want to eat, you Brahmans come out of the temple!"

"We'd rather die! We are nothing more than our caste! We'd rather jump into the river and bash our heads against the asphalt rocks!"

"No one will eat. No one will eat anywhere!"

Shouts came from all sides. Five different groups of men and women and children gathered in five different corners of the farm around the temple.

The Prince cried at the top of his voice.

"O you bastards of Indian Culture! Come and eat or else this might be your last meal.

> Thy flames when driven by the wind, O Agni,
> Disperse, O pure one, pure in all directions;
> And thy divine Navagvas, most destructive,
> Lay low the woods and devastate them boldly
> Or we will be driven and dead.

We will be driven and dead!"

He ran into the temple, followed by his brothers. They did not know what would happen next, but they knew they would have to follow him.

"Go away, go away!" the temple priest shouted. "You've touched the plates of the untouchables. You can't come back and touch our plates now!"

"I'll touch you, I'll touch them, I'll touch them all!"

And then the young Master touched each Brahman's feet and grabbed him and hugged him.

That should never have been done.

"Desecration! Desecration! The end of the world is here! The end of all civilizations and categories and order and sense is here! It's here in the person of this monster crazed by grief. Away, away, away, you pestilence of modern times! O dear God, we've lost our caste! Quick, run, run from him into the bushes, into the thorns and the broken stones. Jump into the river and be purified before sunset. Or else darkness, sin and this devil, this Saturn in the body of a Brahman, will grip us."

They ran wildly and in so doing they bumped into each other and tripped all over. They recovered themselves in shock even as they touched each other, which they were not supposed to do before they finished their meal. They panted and cried and groaned; and some cried profusely. They fell on the thorns. They rushed. Noses held tight, eyes closed, chantings repeated, they threw themselves into the river from every rock, tree and boulder that they could get to. The River. The River. It was the only refuge.

The Prince followed them. "No, no, no, no, sirs, no! I can run faster than you, I can run farther than you. I'll touch you. I'll touch you in a way that you never can deny; that you will have to acknowledge. You'll not deny me. And you'll not escape me!"

He leaped and jumped towards the northwestern side of the river—the side from which the river was coming down. His feet were covered with mud from the crevices of the river ground. The embankments had eroded considerably. He jumped. He fell. He ran again, faster than them all.

The pyre burnt slowly. He shouted and chanted and ranted and sang.

> Cantilena.
> Non-being then existed not, nor being;
> There was no air, nor sky that is beyond it.
> What was concealed? Wherein? In whose protection?
> And was there deep unfathomable water?

He sprang and hopped from rock to rock until he reached the absolute center boulder of the river where there was a statue of the monkey god, Hanuman, emerging out of the river stone, supposedly a miraculous happening of a thousand years ago.

From the boulder he could see the river filled with scores and scores of Brahmans. Priests and archbishops and apprentice worshippers were bathing frantically, offering libations, and cleansing themselves without cease, and hoping against hope that the sun would not set.

He chanted and screamed even as the river drowned his chanting:

> Death then existed not, nor life immortal;
> Of neither night nor day was any token.
> By its inherent force the One breathed windless;
> No other thing than that beyond existed.

Darkness there was at first, by darkness hidden
Without distinctive marks, this all was water.
That which, becoming, by the void was covered,
That One by force of heat came into being.

A priest waded towards the Prince, who was desecrating the boulder by standing so close to the god's statue after having so recently touched an untouchable's dinner plate.

"Haven't you done enough, young man? Do not desecrate the boulder and do not desecrate the river! Can't you understand that the river is the only means we have of purifying ourselves?"

"I will not desecrate," he told the priest with the mesmerizing eyes. "I will not taint. I'll let you all decide what this is all about. What I am going to do now is to relieve myself from here. My water will mix with all the water of the Bhima, the Ganga of the South, all the water that you are bathing in. You decide then if it is purifying or not. You decide then if it is holy or not. After I have relieved myself, you decide if you are truly clean or not."

Then he threw his dark red shawl into the water. It drifted on and on in the languid air. He took off his pure white silk dhoti, tied a stone to it and pushed it down into the river.

There he was, naked and solid and magnificent as the world-famous, sunburned statue of Gomatesvara! Naked and imposing! He relieved himself.

Police Marya watched from the sidelines. "My father told me this would happen, but I did not know it would happen in my own lifetime. The Brahman is destroying the Brahman. The end of the world is perhaps somewhere near the river. The young Master has violated the rule of God. Long time ago I told him not to. I told him not to ask me to. This will be his end. I am sorry. I like the little boy but he's a victim of his fate; his karma."

The river grew darker and darker. Soon it was night. The Brahmans knew that they had stayed in the river too long. They filed back along the narrow and muddy paths towards the temple.

The Prince followed them. He was on top of the southern embankment. He could see, a little distant, the five-tiered chariot that the people used to drag round and round the temple, in holy circles, the God in the highest balcony, the priest holding the offerings on the fourth tier, his children with flowers and fruits in the third tier, and the lower two tiers always empty. And the lower-caste people drew the chariot round the temple with their arms, the heavy 3,000-pound vehicle needing all the forces that could be harnessed to it. Bullocks and buffaloes were supposed to be used only for human transportation. It would have been desecration to use animals for the transportation of gods and priests.

The Prince saw the contours of the God's chariot in the darkness. "Thimma," he shouted. "Thimma, you damned untouchable, my father's other son! I want light. Show me some light this way so I can walk. Ask the servants to run to the village and fetch the kerosene lamps and petromax lamps from the merchant's store!"

"Storeman Nagayya refuses!" someone shouted in the distance.

The young man's body was tired. He sat down on the solitary stone near the chariot.

Thimma rushed. In the distance the slow fire continued to burn, diminishing the Master's body. Thimma hastened to talk to all the servants. They ran towards the village at his behest.

The people waited. And watched. The meal cooled gradually. But no one moved to eat it.

In fifteen minutes the dim lights were near the temple. Thimma had cajoled Nagayya into a compromise. The servants carried the petromax lamps on top of their dirty turbans so they could throw as much light around the countryside as possible.

The countryside was alight with dim white and brown lamps. The Prince asked that one of the petromax lamps be set on the God's chariot. He climbed on the first tier. No one had ever occupied that position before. The first was the lowest of all the tiers.

His father had always addressed the people indirectly. First he listened with care to all that the people had to say. And then he usually let them know of his decisions, always indirectly, through people like Thimma. Only the intermediaries told the people what the Master had done.

In the Prince's consciousness were alit his father's ways. But now he had to handle the hundreds all together.

He was a Brahman. The incantation must undo what the incantation had done. The Vedas must help him reconcile.

"I am and I'm not a Prince. I order you and I beg you to eat together. Sit, sit next to each other!

Darkness there was at first, by darkness hidden;
Without distinctive marks, this all was water.
That which, becoming, by the void was covered,
That One by force of heat came into being.
Dim though it may be, let there be light, please!

They sat down to eat, one next to the other. Thimma's son, Hanumantha, grabbed a place right next to a clean-shaven girl of fourteen, a Brahman girl who had been widowed recently due to the death by consumption of her eighteen-year-old, apprentice-worshipper husband.

They ate in silence. They could not see clearly what they were eating. They did not want to. The light was dim and cast many shadows.

But not one person in the crowd liked the sight of the untouchable Hanumantha sitting next to the adolescent Brahman widow!

Every caste was sullied and displaced. Everyone present at The Meal was angry.

Everyone except Thimma. Thimma cried at the young man's predicament. He wept as the Master's earthly remains slowly went up in flames.

26
finale

THE NEXT DAY THE PRINCE'S brothers returned to town. They begged the Prince to return with them to Hyderabad.

He could not do that. While their carts went towards the railway station, he returned inward, receded further into the country, back to the Mansion. There was still the matter of scattering his father's ashes in the river. He would have to wait until day after tomorrow to gather them. The fire burnt slowly. He must go back and stay in the Mansion for the two nights before the final ceremony.

The Mansion. His final contact with his father. And his grandfather, the man who was assassinated at age thirty-two, in 1908. There would be no member of the family in the house tonight except himself. All alone. That was the way he wanted it for today. That was the only way he could think and be in intimate touch with it all.

The Prince rested alone in the East bedroom on the second floor of the Mansion. He let his mind wander. This was the room where he had spent summer after summer. Lazy afternoons, in the hiatus between the morning work of inspecting the farms and the evening work of meetings with peasants to solve problems on his father's behalf. This room had been his refuge, his beloved niche. Alone but not lonely, watching the distant horizon of trees, and the train to Bombay disappearing in the afternoon summer haze, day after day, he had read and reread the authors who had come to mean so much to him. Jane Austen, Thomas Hardy, Marcel Proust, Thomas Mann, Yasunari Kawabata, Nagai Kafu, Vicente Aleixandre, Odysseus Elytis, Jorge Luis Borges, Pablo Neruda, James Joyce, Tennessee Williams, William Butler Yeats, John Steinbeck, Leo Tolstoy, Arthur Miller, Alberto Moravia, and above all, André Malraux. All those foreign authors who meant so much to him!

Now, the day after his father's funeral, the books were still here, lined up so neatly with markings from summers.

HE was gone but the books were still here.

He thought of his father, and the most important story in his father's life—the story of the loss of his father.

It had been a full-moon night then as it was tonight. His grandfather had been invited to come to a moonlight dinner at the mango orchard, five miles from the Mansion. His last one. His people had warned him not to go. A certain conspiracy was in the air and treachery, deceit and chaos seemed imminent. "Do not go," his wife had implored him. But, in the countryside, not to go would have been equal to death. What the people valued most was courage, extraordinary courage of which they themselves were not capable.

For years, with extraordinary courage and superb planning, grandfather had combined seduction with acquisition. He had seduced every woman of property in the countryside; every woman who possessed legal rights to property that had once belonged to his family, which was all the land extending the length and breadth of the Bhima River delta. Property that had once belonged to his father (the Prince Vishnoo's great-grandfather) and that was lost now, at the beginning of the twentieth century, due to the chicanery and legal trickery of the lawyers and predators who had consistently taken advantage of the fatal weakness in his father—the fatal weakness of complete trust in others. Such trustingness and his own personal integrity had made him blind to the immoral forces around him. His personal word was as good as his deed, and so he saw in others what was only in him. He equated their words with their deeds and took them at their word. That cost him and the family almost all they had. It fell to *him* to set things right; to regain the vast property.

But now, the Prince's grandfather had recovered what was rightfully his family's—not by law or technical legal means, but by charming the sari off any woman with whom he had come in contact —maiden, bride, widow; adolescent, adult, old person; Brahman, Lingayat, Reddy, Kamma or Vaisya.

Most people of means in the countryside associated loss of property with loss of virtue and vice versa. For propertied people in the Deccan, cuckoldry was of two distinct kinds. But the remedy, the answer for the two problems was only one: revenge.

The Prince's grandfather knew that. But if he did not go to the dinner, to that extent he could not rule, he could not be a father to his people. So he went on his fine white steed that matched the milky whiteness of the vast countryside that was totally his now— the countryside and the distant rocks in the river that appeared so white in the full moon.

O grandfather!

The dinner was grand. In the orchard by the distant stream full of hidden mineral springs, they entertained him lavishly. Food, drink and hashish were aplenty. He was a liberated Brahman, a man who combined in himself the intelligence of a priest with the rich living and the controversial morality of a prince.

Too, in the tent by the mango trees, there was a beautiful, fair, untouchable woman named Ganga.

In the moonlight, the trees cast shadows from which he would not emerge. Until satisfied.

And then at midnight he was on his way back to the Mansion. But at the crossing near the stream that divided the states of Karnataka and Andhra Pradesh, his horse slipped and foundered and began to sink in the mud. It had been a deliberate and extremely well-planned tampering with the crossing. Before he could pull his horse out of it, twelve dacoits, hired to come all the way from the jungles of Dandakaranya in central India, pounced on him with daggers, knives, swords and the ax. The fatal blow and the thirty-two-year-old man disappeared forever into the midnight Deccan air like an aspiration that never was. Head was separated from body and buried deep, deep in the crevices forming themselves at the turn where the stream met the river.

The dacoits hid the head and demanded sixty pounds of gold for its return. Being Hindus, they knew that no Hindu funeral rites could be performed to their end unless body and head were together.

So there was a price on his grandfather's head even after his body and head were severed. It took eight days to put body and head together; to pay the ransom, so that the last rites could be performed and the ashes properly scattered in the river.

"Oh my God! How did it all happen?" the Prince shouted in extreme fright.

He turned around in fear, and the sight in front of him now was even more unreal and terrifying. Three men from the middle castes, shining dark, with gleaming teeth (brushed so vigorously, day after day, with the legendary Deccan neem tree sticks), wielding axes, laughed and grinned at him. Their voices were hysterical with pent-up passion.

"Aha! Aha! Aha! Aha! Yesterday's prince! Today's nobody! You forced us to eat our meal all together, didn't you? Aha, aha, look at this man! Property, sex, caste they are all one and the same, boy. One means the other without a doubt! Maybe the boy's right after all! There's nothing wrong in violating rules and order. Maybe there's nothing to these princes, these masters! These are just flesh and blood and weak bodies just like us. That boy's right. If he is any example, perhaps there is no caste system!"

The second man interjected: "But look at the devil! Will you look at the devil? All those books in those weird tongues! This devil raped our society yesterday, just as his grandfather raped all the Deccan women longtime ago. And now we have no one below us!"

"And what happened to his grandfather, may I ask?" the third one said.

"What happened to his grandfather?" they asked each other, knowing the answer full well. They were deep into their dangerous game.

The laughter increased. And the people increased also. Suddenly they were everywhere. Boys, children, grown-up men, doddering old men. From every caste in the countryside. They were on the parapets around the inner courtyard. They were on top of the pink marble high-seat on the terrace. They were in the *Divan-e-Aam*. They were in the *Divan-e-Khas*. Scores of people, with any weapons they had been able to muster. They scurried into the inner chapel of the Mansion—the dark God's room. They opened windows that had been closed for years. Dust and soot and mud began to pour down. The bulls in the stables became restless and hopped and jumped over the giant, tiered haydrawers and down into the low pond. Enraged and confused by the commotion, the Prince's favorite bull, Thimma, jumped the wrong way and fractured its leg.

The stampede began.

Everyone attempted to sit on every prohibited seat, including the old Master's favorite mahogany lounging chair.

"The sacrifice," they cried. "The sacrifice. The sacrifice of the bastard of Indian culture who tells us death is life and life is death."

"The sacrifice," they cried.

Men armed with rural sharpstone slingers took positions on every parapet, every cupola of the Mansion.

"The barn," someone shouted. "The barn is too high this year. Burn the barn. For there must be a fire before a sacrifice. But don't let an untouchable touch it. And don't you be touched by an untouchable!"

And then they dragged the Prince up to the terrace.

The moon was high and clear. The Prince had done something right this year. Early this year he had assumed complete charge of the estate's financial matters, to help his father. He was a good financial manager. Because of good crops well preserved by the Prince, the barn stood unusually high this year. On the southside, though, the devastated mango orchard lay desolate and sparse trees cast lonely night shadows. Far, far away in the West was the Bhima River. The moon made it seem farther than it was. In the north were the homes of prosperous Muslims, and their graves. In the East, far away, winding its way like a matchbox play train, was the early-morning train from Bombay to Madras. Soon it would reach Krishna railway station.

The untouchables watched in glee. And in fear. They were not allowed to, they were not ready to, participate in this Revolution.

Police Marya's fourteen-year-old half-brother, Huccha, poured kerosene all over the high barn. The animals were going wild. The women had climbed to the tops of their homes to watch.

The fire lit within an instant. They began throwing books into the fire—*Pride and Prejudice, Residence on Earth, Thousand Cranes, Snow Country, Fervor of Buenos Aires, The Dynasty, A Portrait of the Artist as a Young Man, Divagations, Büddenbrooks, Death in Venice, Man's Fate, A la recherche du temps perdu,* the Australian A.L. Basham's classic *Cultural History of India* and Mazumdar's *A History of India in Three Volumes.*

One by one the books reached the flames.

"Look, look at what you have done to us!" they shouted as they pushed him to the edge of the terrace. "Ten rupees for a kick! Ten rupees for a slap! The game is called 'Slap the Prince!' We never played the game at the June fair, did we?"

"Can we owe you also this money?" one man asked. "We mean we *owe* you nearly everything else."

"We all owe money to the Prince. If we don't, our fathers did! Let us owe it to *him!* We owe it to *him!*"

As they lifted him high up in the air on all fours and motioned him back and forth a little beyond the Mansion wall and towards the artesian well and back again to the terrace, the Prince's head began to reel. They played back and forth, making ceaseless gestures of throwing him towards the fire once and towards the well the other time.

"You ever fucked an untouchable girl, little Prince?" one man asked. "You talk of touching everybody. They're real good to touch. You know what I mean?"

They dropped him on the terrace floor and he slid all the way on the white marble from one end to the other and bumped his head against the highseat. He scraped his nose, his forehead and his mouth.

And they began pounding on the fallen man. With feet and fist. Human bodies touched him left and right.

"No one can come to the terrace," shouted Police Marya's half-brother Huchha, as he slung stones at the people in the outer courtyard.

A stone hit Sali Thimma as he ran towards the Mansion. He tore a part of his soiled dhoti and tied it on his head. He rushed in, steady and determined.

The people gave way to him. His speed, his decision, his authority stilled them for a minute. They saw that he was bleeding.

He ran from the pedestal into the *Divan-e-Aam*, on to the first and the second floors and finally up to the terrace.

He flung his hands straight out like two sharp axes. His rage was clear, and coming across. His eyes were bloodshot.

"Is there any true son of his mother in this crowd? Let him come! Come on! Come on! Come and touch me! I'm not afraid of dying! Come and touch me and you'll be dead not only here but in the next world forever and ever. Come, come, come and touch the untouchable. I believe in the caste system. And when you believe in something you gain a power that will touch others and destroy them if need be. You come and touch me, I ask you. Anyone who wants to! And let's find out what will happen then. Touch the untouchable! Come on!"

They shrank from him as from a five-headed cobra.

He knelt down and he cried.

"O my poor master! Little boy! You and I are one today. O

Master, forgive me for touching you. O dear God, forgive this Thimma for touching Vishnoo! Perhaps this is the moment of my reincarnation!"

The Prince was unconscious.

Thimma lifted him up on his shoulders. The young Master was limp and heavy.

They shuddered to see the untouchable and the Brahman touching each other; so close and together.

He walked slowly as he looked around at the Mansion that he had never seen so clearly and so intimately before.

The Mansion had been devastated.

Thimma walked down the steps to the *Divan-e-Aam,* then on to the courtyard and beyond. The village dog followed him.

"I could not protect you, young Master, as the old Master wanted me to. I could not protect you from yourself. I have betrayed him. But I hope I have saved you. I hope this man worse than death has given you life. I hope my love has reached out and touched you even as I have resisted touching you, holding you, hugging you, and loving you, all my life. I did not feed you even once in my house even though I always wanted to, so much! If our souls can be one, this old man and you, Thimma and Vishnoo, the Harijan and the Brahman have become one today. You cannot walk up to the terrace any more, Master. You have become an untouchable, just like me. You cannot come back to the villages any more, little Master. Not for a long time. The violence, the change without purpose are here to stay for a while. O Master, you shouldn't have!"

He carried the young man beyond the stream.

The Mansion was becoming more and more distant. Thimma could still hear the shouts, the pandemonium.

They reached the mango orchard. The stars above were clear and bright. Thimma looked up to see if he could see the face of the Master among them, some sign of blessing from heaven. His grief-stricken mind could not decide if part of the Master were still on the earth or if all of it had migrated to *Vaikunth* already.

They reached the Village Robbed. Thimma paused for an instant at his father's grave. He laid the young man on top of it and bent down to drink water from a small canal he had dug. He could clearly hear the sounds, the rumblings of the river. He stood up and looked at the countryside. Way down was the river, clear and placid under the full moon.

Before it was time for the morning train to arrive, Thimma
had reached the railway station.

"You better get the Brahman priest again," said the doctor.
"Your young Master has to go back to the villages. To the Mansion."

Thimma heard what he did not want to hear.

By noon Thimma was at the Saint's shrine by the river. He
laid the young Prince down three yards from the five-tiered God's
chariot.

The shrine bells moved gently in the slowly drifting river air.
They created a simple rhythm.

The fair-complexioned priest with the mesmerizing eyes was
seated peacefully on the high stone wall facing the river. In an even
keel he was chanting invocations from the Vedas and the *Garuda
Purana*.

"O Brahman! Please help me."

"Sit down, Thimma. What can I do?"

"He was a decent, dignified, good young man, sir!"

"Was? What do you mean was?"

"He is dead, sir. Vishnoo is dead."

The day before the Master's funeral the fair-complexioned
priest with the mesmerizing eyes had denied compassion to the
Prince.

At the Mansion he had said, "I must insist unequivocally that
the little Prince be judged on his ability to be a Prince! Today! On
his ability to be a little Master; a person who can demonstrate
unquestioned wisdom to hold together forever society, life and
death in their predestined stark balance."

But today the Prince's death shook him visibly. He was com-
passionate, charitable.

"It did happen, didn't it, Thimma! O dear God! The boy did
not understand."

"He was not much younger than you, sir!"

"Yes, but he did not know. Those he wanted to change considered him not a mover but a breaker of society. A universal truth,
Thimma. People just do not want to live without a hierarchy that

assures safety; each one's relative importance in the order of things."

"Dear sir! The young Prince at least deserves a princely funeral!"

"You are an intelligent man, Thimma! Is that possible now? After what he did two days ago, there can be no princes in the Deccan. And no princely funeral. The people will never come. This Brahman has been touched by an untouchable. This Prince did not want to be a Prince. I am sorry. No one will come. Not the Brahman. Not the middle-caste man. Not the untouchable. Why? Why such absolute defiance?"

"He could not help himself. He was that kind of man."

"And he has met his destiny. O dear God. The fire will not burn him. Agni, the god of fire, will not bless him."

"Can you not help, Brahman?"

"How can I? He broke society's form; form which is order. He broke society's pattern; pattern which is control. He decided to equalize. But that was neither his destiny nor his place."

The priest choked slightly. Thimma observed the priest; his holding back.

"His destiny was always to be either more or less. He was more *then*. He is less *now*, Thimma. Less. Lessened to us."

"Let me seek his brothers, sir!"

"Don't! Don't do that! Or else you may destroy them too."

"You are right, sir! I cannot afford that last betrayal of the old Master."

The priest was silent. Disturbed.

"What do I do now, sir?"

"The river. Let the river take him. Let the river submerge him. Let the river purify him. May God be with you."

"Thank you, sir. Goodbye."

Thimma sat by the thorn trees.

"The little Prince's body has to be let go. I cannot keep it on the ground forever. Bodies have to be let go."

"Let him go, Thimma!"

"I don't want to. He was my little Master. A young child who idealized *me*. My friend. How can I accept that Vishnoo is dead?"

"You must, Thimma."

Night gathered slowly.

Thimma undressed the Prince.

He lowered him gently into the central flow of the river, the flow that always made the curve faster than the rest of the river.

In the distance a light came on at the Saint's shrine as it had every night for the past three hundred years; since the day in the seventeenth century when the Saint had been canonized. The merchant caste men had not failed in their duty. They supplied the oil and the labor.

Farther away, lonely, with a single giant lamp on its parapet, was the Mansion.

"Neither a pyre nor a grave! Neither a Brahman nor an untouchable! What happened to you, little Prince!"

The body floated swiftly. Swifter than he had expected.

Only the land! The land remained. The land that always gave the appearance of merging with the river. The Deccan, flat, infinite, stretched forever.

"Dear God! It is lonely in the Deccan! Oh let it rain, God!"

It rained.

Designed by Barbara Holdridge
Composed in Bodoni Book by ComCom,
    Allentown, Pennsylvania
Printed on 55-pound Glatfelter Supple Offset
    by Maple Press Company, York, Pennsylvania
Bound in Devon Green and Permalin Pumpkin,
    Burnished Leather Grain, with Multicolor
    Antique Russet endpapers, by Maple Press
    Company, York, Pennsylvania
Jackets color-separated and printed by Capper, Inc.,
    Knoxville, Tennessee